RED ROWANS
IN GLEN ORRIN

By the same Author

THE DOCTOR
MORE ABOUT THE DOCTOR
THE DOCTOR CALLS AGAIN
THE DOCTOR AND HIS FRIENDS
FROM A COTTAGE IN PENNYCOOK LANE
THE ADVENTURES OF ELIZABETH GRAY
HELEN ROSE AND THE CHILDREN
GILLIAN MUNRO
WHITE BELL HEATHER
GORRY
BOYSIE
THE STREET OF THE SPINNERS
ANGUS, OUR PRECENTOR
FOLK OF THE GLEN
THE BUT AND BEN
TATTERED TARTAN

RED ROWANS
IN GLEN ORRIN

by

ISABEL CAMERON

LUTTERWORTH PRESS
LONDON

Printed in Great Britain by The Whitefriars Press Ltd.
London and Tonbridge

CONTENTS

1.	RED ROWANS	9
2.	THE SHOOTING PARTY . . .	16
3.	THE *CEILIDH*	23
4.	ALICE	35
5.	"BIDDY"	41
6.	HECTOR MACAULAY	54
7.	THE ROMANCE OF WAR . . .	66
8.	CRANBERRY JAM	72
9.	THE GHILLIES' BALL	84
10.	"MELODION NANNIE" . . .	89
11.	BURIED TREASURE	94
12.	CALLUM	100
13.	KIRSTY CAMPBELL, SALESWOMAN . .	111
14.	THE ELEVENTH HOUR . . .	126
15.	THE GAELIC STUDENT . . .	136
16.	HEATHER ALE	146
17.	THE HIKERS' BOTHY	153
18.	FEBRUARY-FILL-THE-DYKES . . .	169

CHAPTER ONE

RED ROWANS

I⊤ was a still, hot morning in September. The girl seated in an ancient garden-chair in front of the cottage door had finished her task of shelling a basketful of late peas. She let her eyes dwell with quiet satisfaction upon her surroundings, looking first at the little garden before her, and then lifting her eyes to the hills.

The hills had wrapped round their shoulders a royal mantle of purple heather; down by the loch side a clump of wood, still green, denied that it was autumn, even when a rowan tree bent forward to gaze admiringly at her crown of scarlet berries! The world refused to believe that winter was coming.

Nearer at hand, within the cottage garden, were a couple of rowan trees, for every Highland home believes that

> " Rowan tree and red threid
>   Send the witches on their speed."

To wear a knot of rowan berries is to be safe from the evil eye. But Elspet MacLeod had tucked a bunch of rowans into the waist-belt of her white overall because she loved their colour.

From the cottage came the heartsome scent of peat reek mingled with an appetising smell of fried venison and onions. Aunt Eppie was preparing dinner, the girl thought. She must go in with the peas.

But still she sat on dreaming. The quiet of the Glen was in her eyes, its gentle brooding on her spirit.

Suddenly the quietness was shattered by the raucous note of a motor horn. The red motor, a rapid-looking little " M.G.," had come to a halt on the road at the foot of the garden, and a tall young man clad in Harris tweed plus-fours was advancing towards her, cap in hand.

" Can you tell me am I far from Orrin Lodge, please ? " he asked.

He spoke with the cultured musical voice of an educated Englishman. Elspet almost forgave him for owning such a noisy motor.

She rose to her feet and stood facing him. She was a tall lass, and with her cropped fair hair, dark blue eyes, and long, white overall she reminded him of a female chorister. By rights she should have been holding a psalter in her hand while out of her mouth should have issued the matchless melody of a Gregorian chant.

But instead she was replying to his question in a voice as soft as the balmy, sunny air. "You are about five miles from the Lodge, sir," she said. "The Lodge is right at the head of the loch. That road," she pointed to the white ribbon running at the end of the garden, "goes up to it, but no farther."

"Thank you very much," he said, and made as if to take his departure. "I suppose there is no place hereabout where a man could get a drink—otherwise than water! I'm desperately thirsty."

"My aunt sells beer," she replied.

"Cheers!"

"Ginger beer, treacle and herb beer," she said, smiling. "She makes it herself. If you come in——" She led the way into the cottage and then he noticed that one end of the little house had been turned into a shop.

"What will you have?" she asked politely, taking her place behind a little counter on which were ranged bottles of home-made brews of various kinds, and tumblers of various sizes.

He examined the bottles. "I think I'll try the treacle beer," he said cautiously.

She motioned him to take a seat on the white-scrubbed bench behind the shop door. Meantime she filled his tumbler and handed it to him.

He took a cautious sip, conscious that she was watching him.

" I suppose you can all make beer hereabout—and whisky ? " he inquired, playing for time, for he was not sure if he liked the taste of this home-made brew. If she'd go away for a moment he would empty the sweet, sticky stuff away. Where, by the way, could he empty it ? There was a brown crock on a low shelf, half-full of water and holding a bunch of red rowans. He'd empty the beer in there—that is—if she'd only go away for a moment.

But Elspet showed no desire to go away. He gulped down another mouthful and tried not to " grue." Then he asked : " May I smoke ? "

" Oh, surely, surely ! " She granted his request. Then she went on : " We—we—sell cigarettes, too."

" By Jove ! I'm in luck ! " he said, heartily. " I'll have a couple of packets, please."

He set down his half-empty glass upon the counter and thrust his hand deeply into his pocket. He brought out a handful of silver and selected enough coins to pay, and more than pay, for his purchase.

" Thank you, sir," she said gratefully, and at the same time she replenished his glass to the brim. " I'm so glad you like the beer," she said simply. " Would you be for a biscuit or a bap to it ? "

" *To* it ? "

" I mean *with* it." From a tin box she unearthed some exceedingly able-bodied-looking scones. " Oh, no," he said politely. " I'll just have the beer and a cigarette."

Miserably he wondered how he was ever to finish the beer !

" Elspet, what are you doing ? " a voice from the back kitchen cried. " It's time you had on the tatties . . . and where's the peas ? "

" Excuse me, sir," Elspet said in her gracious Highland way. She was much more a hostess than a shopkeeper. " Will you just fill up the glass yourself ? There's still almost half a bottle left. I must speak to my aunt. I'll get your change, too."

The moment he was alone he emptied the beer into the crock. What the effect would be on the rowans he neither knew nor cared. He must depart, and right quickly, too. If

13

that quiet-eyed lass (who looked like a female chorister) returned, he could see himself swallowing all the beer to its last drop rather than hurt her feelings.

He could hear voices talking in the back kitchen, and once he was almost sure someone laughed—a mischievous, girlish laugh. It couldn't be the chorister, he mused, and stooped to pull the ears of a cocker spaniel that had come to make friends with him.

The spaniel had a ball and proposed that he and the young man should have a game. " But I can't wait, old man," the motorist protested.

" Have you finished your beer already, sir ? " Elspet was back again, grave-eyed, serious, and hospitable. " I must give you your change."

" No, no, I don't want the change. Keep it, please. And thank you very much for your kindness—I'm most grateful. Good morning." And lifting his cap he hurried down the garden path. One would almost have thought he was flying from some danger, so swiftly did he " step on the juice " of the red " M.G." and send her tearing along the road.

The girl watched him thoughtfully. Then

she went into the little shop, examined the empty bottle and glass and sniffed around suspiciously. Guided by her nose, she discovered the crime.

" My poor rowans," she said, tenderly, and carried them away to have the water changed.

CHAPTER TWO

THE SHOOTING PARTY

ORRIN LODGE, where Sir Hugh MacPherson had gathered his shooting friends, was literally " at the back of beyond." Even the public road vanished into a heathery track where sheep strayed and rabbits scampered. Angry grouse cried, " Go back, go back," and it was rumoured that at the Muckle Cairn by the riverside a family of foxes had their home. A couple of eagles quartered the moor and herds of deer bounded up the hillside, pausing sometimes to look down defiantly at the human beings who sought to end their beautiful lives.

The air was heady with the scent of bog myrtle and honey as the shooting party set out.

" Is it dangerous work, Mr. Blake ? " a town-bred girl asked the motorist who owned the " M.G." which his sporting friends described as a " snappy piece of work " and christened " Red Biddy."

" Not a bit, Miss Miles," he answered. " You come with me. I'll promise not to shoot you."

Alice Miles was timid. It was her first shooting party, and though she loved Scotland and the Scots she said she'd feel safer with Mr. Blake than with a Scotsman.

" But *I am* a Scot," he protested. " My mother was one of the Robertsons of Struan," he glared at her triumphantly.

" Is that so ? " Alice said sweetly. She had never heard of the Robertsons of Struan, and she only hoped they were quite respectable. Their young descendant was, of that she was sure. Robert Blake, high up in the home Civil Service, with private means and no encumbrances, was not only respectable but desirable !

Alice had a sweet smile. Her friends described her as a sweet girl. She said it made her shudder to see poor, helpless creatures slaughtered. All the same, she wore a blackcock's feather in her felt hat and her tiepin had certainly once been the left foot of a ptarmigan. And only poverty prevented her from wearing a real sealskin coat.

The shooting party was a fairly large one, and after much discussion it was decided that the ladies should join the sportsmen and have lunch with them at one o'clock in Birchwood.

Lady MacPherson, looking smart and business-like in her "tailor mades," with tweed hat and gaiters to match, shouldered her gun and set out with the men, leaving the others to follow in the big motor-car.

Miss Campbell, who came from Lochaber and who, it was rumoured, could sing Gaelic songs, drove the sports car with much pleasure to herself and much trepidation to her passengers. As the road was narrow and twisty they heaved sighs of relief when they reached the trysting-place.

The shooting party, looking keen but hungry, were waiting for them, and when rugs and motor-car cushions had been collected they all seated themselves and began a spirited attack upon an enormous lunch which would have rejoiced the heart of a Pickwick party.

" Even bread and cheese eaten out of doors tastes ever so much better than *hors-d'œuvre*," Jock MacKintosh said. He was the Laird's nephew and heir. He had a red, happy face and a good-natured laugh. He spoke with his mouth full and was immediately rebuked for his bad manners by Lady MacPherson, who was eating a hunk of bread so thick she had to attack it sideways.

" Have some wine ? " someone asked, speaking, like the March Hare, in an encouraging tone.

Alice Miles, to whom the invitation was given, looked all round. " I don't see any wine," she said.

" There isn't any." Alice, who did not know her namesake of Wonderland, was annoyed when the others laughed.

Because Robert Blake was sorry for Alice Miles with her sweet, timid smile, he began to tell with great gusto his experiences in the little shop where they sold beer and cigarettes. He made the party roar with laughter as he described his despair when the " female chorister," as he called her, filled up his glass just as he was congratulating himself upon emptying it.

" What did it taste like ? " Jock MacKintosh asked.

" It had a taste like burnt toffee, and a smell like shoe varnish with a dash of treacle in it, and it looked like soapy dish-water."

" Sounds intriguing," said David Keith, who was a lawyer and came from Edinburgh. " I propose we go and visit the shop and get some of these beers."

" What was the girl like ? " Alice wanted to know.

" If we are to discuss ladies' looks we'll get no shooting done this afternoon," Sir Hugh said hastily. Robert Blake shot him a grateful look and the party began at once folding up rugs and replacing motor cushions.

Alice Miles, who was feeling cold and rather cross, was not enjoying her first shooting party. In the bottom of her heart she wished she were at home with her feet on the fender and a novel in her hand.

" You come with me, Miss Miles," Robert Blake said. " Here, give me your hand and I'll help you over the cart track. I hope you're enjoying yourself? Don't the hills look fine in the sunshine? "

" They're just sweet," she gushed, after which conversation languished.

" Now take shelter at my back and don't speak or move," Blake cautioned her when they reached the butt.

She threw him an arch glance and tried to stamp her feet, which were full of pins and needles. But much was at stake; she'd endure more than mere physical discomfort for the pleasure of taking shelter behind Robert Blake's square shoulders.

" I like the smell of your Harris tweed," she murmured.

" Hush ! " he whispered.

There was a delightful sense of intimacy in this silent waiting for something to happen. From far off came the cry of the beaters. Nearer and nearer it came ; there was a whirr of wings, the guns began to speak, the twigs cracked, and then death, sudden and, one hopes, painless to innumerable lovely creatures.

A hare squealed—it was a sickening sound. Sir Hugh, with a rapt expression on his lean, weather-beaten face, was blazing furiously and missing seldom. Robert Blake was equally intent.

Alice, tucked in at his back, was bored stiff. She could see nothing—what she heard was not pleasant, and her feet were dead. Tears of self-pity filled her blue eyes.

" I'd like to go home," she whispered.

The drive was over, so Robert could spare time to look over his shoulder at his companion. " You poor little thing," he said, compassionately.

" I—I—hated to see the poor things killed," she sobbed.

Robert, deeply contrite, said : " I suppose we men are still savages at heart." She was sobbing bitterly by this time. . . . Well, well, what man ever yet disliked a tender-hearted

woman ? Robert comforted her to the best
of his ability ; he wiped her tears with a hanky
that smelled of tobacco and gunpowder ; he
put an arm round her shaking shoulders and
bitterly reproached himself for being such a
heartless brute. He called her a " poor little
thing," though she was a tall girl.

That evening Alice concluded that, after
all, her first shooting party had been a great
success. The party were going in a body to a
Gaelic concert in the village the following
evening and Robert Blake had specially invited
her to share " Red Biddy " with him.

CHAPTER THREE

THE *CEILIDH*

THE village hall was already crowded when the party from Orrin Lodge arrived. Two pipers in the barbaric but beautiful Highland dress marched up and down outside the hall, the skirl of their pipes setting feet " tramping time " to the infectious tune of " Stirling Castle."

Sir Hugh and Jock MacKintosh wore kilts with sporrans of badgers' skins—there is nothing so lucky. Lady MacPherson looked dignified in black satin with touches of vivid green, true colours of the Gael. Alice Miles was girlish and unsophisticated in a white dress, and out of compliment to Scotland she wore a tartan sash. It was a fancy tartan unknown to any clan, but that was a mere trifle. Kirsty Campbell wore a gay dress of orange and grey with ornaments of tawny cairngorms which suited her peculiar type of red-haired beauty.

The hall was adorned with stuffed deers' heads, their glassy eyes gazing disdainfully over the heads of the audience. Great bunches of heather were placed in the windows and the stone mantelpiece blazed with red rowans. By one side of the open hearth was a spinning-wheel, on the other a clarsach (Celtic harp). Peats blazed on the hearth, and in a corner, hidden almost out of sight, was a piano.

"Is this the way you always have concerts?" Alice asked, and Kirsty Campbell replied: "You poor, silly Sassenach—this isn't a concert—this is a *ceilidh*, and here is the bard himself coming to preside."

An old Highlander had just entered and the pipes roared a welcome.

The talk was all in Gaelic and bewildering, but out of deference to those who did not know the language the bard (his other name was Torquil MacPhail) announced that Mr. Murdo Macfarlane would sing a song.

Murdo, a humorous-looking fellow, sang with immense gusto the "Wedding of John Bain's Sister." Roars of laughter greeted each verse, and by the time the singer had reached the last verse those who knew the song were lustily joining in.

An old woman—a "cailleach"—with a snowy mutch on her head and a tartan shawl pinned round her shoulders—sang in a sweet old voice a spinning song, the whirr of the wheel being her only accompaniment.

" Well done, Shenag," said the bard, clapping her on the back. " Your voice is as lovely as it ever was."

Then someone threw on more peats, lights were lowered, and a tall, slim girl sat down beside the clarsach and with a sweep of her slender arm she transported her listeners to the misty islands of the west.

" Last Night by the Shieling " was the title of her song, and the melody was a haunting one made memorable by the soft, sympathetic chords of the harp.

" You must sing to us again, my lass," the bard cried, his face bright with excitement. " And now, if you please, Alistair Gow will recite to us one of his own poems." Lights were raised.

Alistair, a lusty young blacksmith, worked himself and his hearers into a state of wild excitement over the doings of a heroic chieftain of the olden days who had gone to battle fasting and lost his head, and who ever after rode, a headless corpse, through the dark woods.

Then the pipers filled the hall with the roars

and skirls of their pipes. " Partners for the Highland Reel " was cried. Seats were thrust back ; a space was cleared and partners chosen ; men and women faced each other, and with wild cries of " hooch " the dance began. Everybody joined in it, music and excitement sending the blood racing through their veins.

Blake, who had been dancing with a rosy-cheeked, black-haired girl, was as wildly excited as anyone. His partner frankly wiping her brow after her exertions, smiled in the most friendly fashion and said : " That was grand ! "

" I like your—what d'you call it ? "

" Our *ceilidh*," the girl said, supplying the strange word and making it sound musical, too.

Blake was still trying to pronounce this Gaelic word when the silver notes of the clarsach sounded through the hall again and everyone held their breath and listened.

The lights were not dimmed this time, so Blake could see the singer. There are two ways in which a Highland woman can look her best : one is at the spinning-wheel, the other is playing the clarsach.

The girl who was seated at this strange old musical instrument wore a dress of some soft green stuff, and tucked into her belt was a bunch of red rowans. Sitting in the glow of the peat fire with the light shining on her fair head and dancing on the chords of her harp, she made an unforgettable picture. So might a queen from Fairyland look and sing and play !

And how she sang ! This time it was " Colin's Cattle," a fairy tune sung first by a human being who had been carried away to Fairyland and who took this way of letting her sweetheart know where she was. Every evening at milking time she sang to the cows.

> " Cro Chalain when wearied
> Wi' the heat o' the day
> Gie doun 'mang the heather
> And their calves roun' them play.
>
> Cro Chalain are bonnie,
> Cro Chalain are dear,
> Grand at fillin' the coggie,
> Sonsie calves they aye rear."

Moved by some force outside themselves the hearers joined in the chorus with spontaneous warmth.

" Who is she ? " Hugh asked his little dance partner.

" Her name is Elspet MacLeod, and she is living in the meantime with her auntie, her that has the little sweetie shop at the loch side."

Robert looked again ; of course it was his female chorister. Well, Scotland was a surprising country. But not so surprising, either, when you remember that the blood of kings still flows in the veins of the Highlanders !

But she was singing again, standing this time while some unseen player accompanied her on the piano, and her song was a heart-gripping one : " O Rowan Tree." The wailing sorrow of it ! The wistfulness and the loveliness of it bespelled her hearers.

When she ceased singing there was a dead silence ; there can be no higher compliment : and then, then—the applause burst forth and made the rafters ring.

" Elspet *m'eudail*," the bard said, looking interrogatively at the singer, " and will you not be giving us another one of your songs, please ? Something cheery this time, something we can all sing and stamp our feet to."

And so she sang " Dance to Your Shadow,"

one of the gayest and daftest of the Gaelic
lilts.

" After we get a cup of tea and a farle of
oatcake we'll have a waulking song," said
the bard.

" Of all the delightful entertainments——"
said Robert.

" Isn't it quaint? " Alice asked amiably.
At first she had been rather annoyed that
Robert had not chosen her for his partner for
the reel, but he had explained that it was out
of deference to her feelings he had spared
her. The mere physical exertion was not for
her !

" That girl who sang last did quite nicely,
didn't she, Mr. Blake? I mean that tall
girl who sang ' O Rowan Tree.' With some
training she might become quite good," she
added kindly, " though it is a pity her arms
are so skinny—they rather spoil her when she
plays the harp."

" Tea, sir? " A cup of exceedingly strong
tea accompanied by buttered bannocks of oatcake was handed to him. The old woman
who had sung the " Spinning Song " was
again busy at her wheel, all around him
voices were friendly and laughter frequent.
In such an atmosphere it did not seem unduly

forward that Robert Blake should recall to Elspet MacLeod their former meeting.

The worst of it was she was in universal demand. Just then she was standing speaking to a tall young Highlander who wore the brave colour of the Seaforths in his kilt. He had a fiddle tucked beneath his arm, and Robert Blake had to admit, though reluctantly, that he was uncommonly good-looking.

" Who is that tall chap speaking to Miss MacLeod ? " Blake asked the bard, to whom he had been introduced earlier in the evening.

" That's Sir Donald MacKenzie of the Seaforths," was the amazing answer.

All unconscious of being watched, Sir Donald tucked his fiddle beneath his chin and softly played a few bars of music. " Is that it, Elspet ? " he asked.

" Not *quite* right. This is how it goes." She hummed the tune. " You see, the ' Iona Boat Song ' must have the rhythm of oars in it."

" I'll come along some evening and we'll try it again," the young man suggested.

" Yes, do, Donald," she replied. " Here's the buttonhole you asked for," she went on, handing him a bunch of red rowans.

" Put it in for me," he coaxed.

She smiled mischievously and said something in Gaelic which made them both laugh as they shared the joke. Robert, hearing them, resolved grimly that he'd learn this language or die in the attempt. Meantime— " Excuse me, Miss MacLeod, I'd just like to thank you once more for directing me to Orrin Lodge."

She looked at him as if she did not remember him, which was very wicked, for she had been conscious of his presence all the evening.

" And did you find your way ? " she asked politely.

" Thanks to you, I did," he said, " and I enjoyed my rest in your cottage."

" And the beer ? " she asked, solemnly.

" Very much." (The audacious liar !)

" I am glad," she said simply, " because it was the wrong stuff I gave you. It was herb beer which my aunt gives to her cows when they are not very well. . . . It does not suit everyone," she went on in her simple, guileless fashion. " A bunch of red rowans I had on the shop counter died of it ! " She opened her dark eyes wide and looked at him to see if he were equally amazed.

" I'm sorry," he said, looking at the rowans

in her belt, " because I'm exceedingly fond of
these berries."

Then he heard once more that laugh,
mischievous and merry, which he had heard
before, and it came from the lips of the
" female chorister."

And this, this princess, was the girl to whom
he had said, patronisingly : " You can keep
the change." The remembrance made his
face hot.

" I must learn Gaelic quickly," he laughed,
" so that I can tell you exactly what I think
of your conduct ! It's a wonder I'm not dead
like the rowan berries."

" People don't die of treacle and Epsom-
salts," she retorted, as she moved away.

Kirsty Campbell gave him his next shock.
He had always imagined Kirsty to be a jolly,
hail-fellow-well-met girl. But, then, he hadn't
heard her sing " Deirdre's Farewell."

She sang it now, and the sorrow, the
ancient sorrow of her people, was in her song.
She sang it unaccompanied, too, and it was
sheer joy to listen to the pure, true notes of her
contralto voice.

" How are all your Celtic songs so sorrow-
ful ? " Blake asked Lady MacPherson.

" That's how we mislead the Sassenach into

thinking we're a sad people," she whispered. "We're not really."

"No," Blake said thoughtfully. "I think you're like your own rowan tree, showing the poor Sassenach your sombre side and keeping the gay berries for yourselves."

"But when we have leaf and berry," she retorted wittily, "we have complete harmony, and when Sassenach meets Celt the same thing happens."

A thick-set man with a bald head and hard blue eyes had just entered the hall. He looked all around as if in search of someone, and then made straight for Elspet MacLeod.

Robert Blake moved off, conscious of a feeling of cold dislike to this newcomer.

"That's Doctor Burgess," the Laird told him. "A man for whom I have a great admiration. He is the only doctor in the Glen that has ever made money! He knows both sides of a penny, and if his patients haven't pennies he takes a couple of fowls or a sheep or a 'cattle beast.' Aye, Doctor Burgess is a hard chap. No, he's not a Highlander; he comes from Fife, and you know the old word says: 'You must have a long spoon if you sup with a Fifer!'"

"Some day next week will suit me; just let

me know which and when," Elspet **was** saying. " All right, Doctor."

" It won't do a particle of good to the old chap," he said, in a voice as unpleasant as his appearance, " but it'll please the old wife, and I'll see about the fees."

CHAPTER FOUR

ALICE

THERE was nothing of the " Nosey Parker " about Alice Miles. She said so herself, so it must have been pure accident that led her the following week to the little shop by the loch side.

She wanted picture post cards, she said, and waxed eloquent on the beauty of the view from the cottage door. She lingered so long over the post cards that Aunt Eppie, who had been attending to her wants, showed distinct signs of impatience.

" Will that be all, mem ? " she asked politely.

Alice looked brightly around. " Cigarettes ? Well, I might have a few packets. They'll come in handy for giving to the gamekeepers and the ghillies."

" They will that," Aunt Eppie agreed. " There was one of the gents from Orrin Lodge in my shop the other day and he bought cigarettes for *himself*."

The sarcasm of this was lost on Alice whose mind was set on seeing the girl who had sung

at the *ceilidh* and in whom Robert Blake
showed a quite unnecessary interest.

" I think Scotland is such a beautiful
country," she gushed, " and your ways are
so—so—you know what I mean ? "

" I couldn't say what you mean," Aunt
Eppie said, unhelpfully.

" Oh, well, unusual—quaint ! We all went
to the concert in the village. It was *such*
fun ! The performers were delightful and the
singing—well, I never heard anything like
it."

" I dare say no'," said Aunt Eppie, wilfully
misunderstanding her.

" One girl sang quite nicely—we were rather
charmed with her singing. She played on the
harp, too. My friend, Mr. Blake, says it's a
pity this girl could not have some good music
lessons, for her voice is quite worth training."

And Elspet, who was in the kitchen, and
had listeners' usual luck, smiled wickedly to
herself.

" It seems a pity, doesn't it ? " Alice went
on brightly. " Still, the audience in the hall
seemed quite pleased."

" And wasn't that a blessing ? " quoth
Aunt Eppie. " That will be four shillings
altogether, mem."

"I could stand all day and look at your lovely landscape," Alice gushed. She had reached the outer door by this time.

"I'm sure if you like it so much you're quite welcome to stay. You can be sitting down in that chair," Aunt Eppie said; "but in the meantime I must go out and feed my hens."

"Was—was—wasn't Mr. Blake here the other day?" Alice was in desperation and had to get her question out. "He's a tall, dark young gentleman and drives a red sports car."

Aunt Eppie considered the matter carefully.

"There was an Indian here on a bike selling silk stockings," she mused. "He was as black as a nigger. Then there was a mannie wanting me to buy a wireless set—he was in a motor-car, but he was fat and bandy-legged. Was that the man you were asking about?"

"Certainly not," Alice said in icy tones. "Why, there he is in his little red car. He said he'd pick me up. Good afternoon," and she was away.

She and her companion were back again next minute. "Cigarettes, please!" Robert

Blake called out cheerily, and then noticing Aunt Eppie's rather grim face he became respectful and polite.

While he was waiting for his cigarettes he, too, looked about for Elspet. He had not seen her since the night of the *ceilidh*, and he was all anxiety to begin the study of Gaelic. He, a Robertson of Struan, to be so ignorant of his mother tongue was deplorable !

He still winced when he recalled the " tip " he had left on the counter. Well, she had no business to look so guileless, for she had been playing tricks on him.

" I suppose you haven't a cocktail shaker ? " Alice asked brightly. " Lady MacPherson's needing one."

Aunt Eppie's face was strictly non-committal. She thought deeply and then asked : " Would a feather duster do instead ? My cock moulted and I collected his tail feathers and made them into a brush for dusting my girdle when I'm baking. If you like, I'll give it to her Leddyship."

Alice looked perplexed. What *was* a girdle, anyway ?

Blake's eyes were dancing with fun. " No, Miss MacLeod," he said. " I don't think a feather duster would do, but it's awfully kind of you to suggest it. Now, young lady," turning to Alice, " have we finished ? "

She nodded thoughtfully. " Don't forget you've promised to give me a motor lesson this afternoon," she reminded him with a sweet smile. " I'd just love to be able to drive ' Biddy.' She's such a ducky little car."

" She's the dickens at times," Blake muttered. Clearly Elspet was not at home, or if she were she must be hiding in the kitchen. Alice did not tell him that she'd caught a glimpse of the long, white overall of the " female chorister " just before she reminded him of her motoring lesson. Besides, how was she to know that Robert Blake was interested in a girl whose aunt kept a sweetie shop ?

Her gay laugh rang out as she entered the car. She sat at the wheel this time and screamed when the engine roared. Blake had to reassure her and to tell her it was all right. He held his capable brown hand over her timid little one, guiding her along the road. The track they left was zigzag.

" Am I doing any better ? " she asked, throwing an appealing look at her teacher.

" Fine, fine," he muttered. " Don't take your eye off the road for a single moment."

Elspet, from the shop window, watched

" Biddy " lurching along like a drunken man. Then she went and looked at her store of lint and sticking-plaster. She also said between her clenched teeth : " *Amadan !* " Now *amadan* is the Gaelic for fool. Who the fool was she did not say.

CHAPTER FIVE

"BIDDY"

" Biddy " belonged to the female sex, therefore she had a temperament. She knew quite well when an alien hand tried to drive her, and she resented it accordingly.

After bucketing about from side to side of the road she took matters in her own hand. Her driver, of course, gave her her opportunity by stepping on the accelerator instead of on the foot-brake. It was all the excuse " Biddy " wished for. With a roar from her engine she flew along the road like a streak of lightning, and at the corner she dashed into a horse and cart, head on.

Both vehicles were upset. On the cart had been a tall zinc drum which contained weed-killer. So violently was it thrown to the ground the drum burst and its contents were splashed on the road. The world became a place full of hideous sounds, creaking brakes, buckling wheels, the terrified neighing of the horse and the cries of the carter.

" Biddy " had turned turtle and had pinned her passengers beneath her red body. In the miraculous way in which a crowd gathers even in a lonely place, half a dozen harvest hands from a near-by field hurried to the rescue. Willing hands lifted " Biddy " and freed her victims. Alice, white-faced and terrified, did not seem hurt, but her companion was unconscious. In trying to gain control of the steering-wheel he had leaned too far over and the wheel had dealt him a stunning blow on the head.

" And the weed-killer is all over his face," said one of the rescue party, wiping off the poison from Blake's face.

" What'll we do now, lads ? " Tom MacKay, the carter, asked. The helpers held a hasty committee meeting, and decided to send the *orra loon* [1] for the doctor, and just at that moment the big sports car belonging to the Lodge appeared on the scene.

Sir Hugh was with them in an instant and took command of the situation. The terrified horse was to be led away, rubbed down and comforted in his stable. Sir Hugh then turned his attention to the other victims. Blake was still unconscious, so very tenderly he was lifted into the back of the car. Alice was helped into the front, and Tom MacKay, the carter, whose

[1] Odd man.

shoulder had been badly wrenched, was given a seat in the middle.

" We'll send a car to tow the ' M.G.' away," Sir Hugh said. " Meantime, one of you men hurry for the doctor, and tell the policeman, too."

Sir Hugh drove very carefully, congratulating himself that the car had been empty, so that Blake could have all the back seat to himself.

" Tell me how it happened," he asked Alice. " Oh, well, never mind," seeing her tears. " You'll tell me all about it when you're feeling better. How have you hurt your hand ? "

" I think it must have been the weed-killer. When the can burst everything was splashed with it. I think I'm burnt."

Sir Hugh knitted his brows in alarm. " I hope it didn't touch your eyes ? "

" Oh, no, only my hand."

" It's horribly poisonous," he said. " I told Tom MacKay to move the drum down to the Home Farm so as to be ready for the spring work. I wish now I hadn't—it would have done quite as well in February."

" Only my hand has been burnt," Alice said gently, and wrapped it in her silk scarf

43

and winced with the pain. Her shrewd little
mind was busily at work all the time. Should
inconvenient questions be asked, this burnt
hand of hers would come in quite useful.
Again she shuddered, but next minute she was
smiling bravely again. " It's nothing," she
murmured. " Poor Mr. Blake ! " Then her
tears fell. " He *would* make me drive."

" By Jove, you're a brave lassie ! " Sir Hugh
said, admiringly.

It was still dark when Blake regained con-
sciousness. Where was he ? What had happened ? And how was it so dark ?

He moved uneasily and found his head was
bandaged. The bandage covered his eyes,
too ; that was the explanation of the darkness.

He put up his hands to push aside the
cotton wool that blinded him, and instantly
someone said : " Don't touch that, please ;
just lie still. The doctor will be here in a
minute."

Blake lay still obediently, and gradually out
of the confusion in his mind memory woke
with all her busy train. " Biddy "—the farm
cart—that awful head-on collision—yes, yes,
he was piecing together the terrible experi-

ences of—when was it ? Yesterday ? Or last year ?

" What happened ? " he whispered. " Who's hurt ? "

" ' Biddy ' seems to have suffered most," the voice said. " Miss Miles' hand is burnt with the weed-killer ; Tom MacKay, the carter, has hurt his shoulder ; the horse is suffering from shock and scratches ; but poor ' Biddy ' is a wreck, physical, mental, yes— and moral, too. I always said that ' M.G.' had no conscience."

" Jock MacKintosh, is it you ? "

" The same, sir," Jock replied briskly, " doing hospital duty till the doctor comes back. I was told to fell you if you tried to undo your bandages."

" You needn't fell me," Blake retorted. " I feel like a chewed boot-string."

" Have something to drink ? " Jock said, holding a feeding cup to Blake's lips and spilling the contents down his neck.

Both men said what they thought about this, and then the door opened. " Oh, Doctor, you're just in time ! The patient is most unruly. Do I fell him as per your orders ? "

Blake felt cool, capable fingers on his pulse,

a hand was slipped below his pillow raising his head gently, and the drinking cup was held to his lips. Thirstily he swallowed the draught, and then his head fell back again, rivers roared in his ears ; now it was an express train tearing down a rocky defile, swinging dizzily in space ; and then a blank.

He was still in darkness when he came to himself again. That was strange, because he could feel the bandages were off his forehead and eyes.

"I can't see," he whispered desperately.

"It will be all right," a voice said comfortingly. "Just shut your eyes. I'm going to put on your bandage again. The room is dark, you know. I've been keeping down the blinds."

"Oh, is that it ? " he said in relieved tones. "I was afraid there was something wrong with my eyes. Are you the doctor ? "

"Yes—Doctor Burgess wasn't at home, so they came for me. I'm an emergency doctor."

"Are—you—are—you—a lady ? "

"Yes." The voice had a lilt of laughter in it now. "Your doctor, though you may not believe it, is a woman."

He pondered this piece of information and

had opened his mouth to ask more questions when she silenced him by sticking the thermometer between his teeth. After she had examined it, she said : " Now go to sleep. I'll be back soon."

" When ? To-morrow ? What day is this ? When did ' Biddy ' run away—the little spitfire ? And how is Alice Miles ? "

She told him the accident had happened two days ago. Her voice was wholly without accent, the voice of an educated Englishwoman, and there is nothing more pleasant to listen to. Yet, now and then, there were fugitive notes in it which reminded him of someone else. Who was it ?

" I've a feeling——" he began.

" So have I," she retorted, " and it is that you must not utter another word. Good-bye just now, Mr. Blake." The soft shutting of the door told him she had gone.

It was a long day, a long, dark day for Robert Blake. Sir Hugh came in breezily, trying to hide his nervous dread of inconvenient questions beneath a flood of small talk. " We're waiting till you're better to have a go at the stags," he said. " Meantime, Jock and I are doing a bit of fishing. We caught a salmon last night—a small fish about five pounds, using the Butcher fly." He thereupon plunged into a perfect torrent of words about the merits of the Butcher versus the Black Jock. " But I'm tiring you, old man," he said, having successfully talked without ceasing for fully ten minutes. " I'll send Jock to sit with you for a while. Did the doctor say anything about ——? "

" No." For some strange reason Robert Blake was seized with panic. " Sir Hugh, what was in the drum that fell on the road ? "

" Weed-killer."

" Poisonous ? "

" Oh, not deadly. Alice Miles got some on her hand and it's almost right again."

" But if it fell on your face or went into your eyes ? "

" Well, it didn't fall on your face or go into your eyes, so why do you ask such stupid questions ? "

Robert Blake was silent. " My face was wet with the stuff," he said quietly, " and my eyes were full of it, too."

" Nonsense ! " Sir Hugh rose noisily to his feet, noisily he cleared his throat, and the closing of the door told Robert Blake he was alone—alone and in the dark with this appalling, terrifying thought to keep him company.

Even to himself he did not dare to utter the
dread word.

Lady MacPherson sat with him that afternoon and read the newspapers. She said she
didn't see why he should not smoke a cigarette,
and unearthed the packet he had bought that
day so long ago in the little shop.

" Who is the lady doctor that is looking
after me ? " he asked suddenly. It was good
the bandages so closely covered his eyes that
he could not see her face as she answered in a
nonchalant voice :

" She's a London doctor who is here on
holiday. She's rather a don at eye trouble. It
was awfully lucky we got her. She's having a
consultation with Doctor Burgess one of these
days on old Hector MacAulay. The poor old
man has cataract on both eyes and she seems
to think something can be done to help
him."

Blake pondered this information in very
much the same way as a dog takes a favourite
bone into his kennel so as to be undisturbed.
There was some mystery. He'd piece the
bits of the puzzle together somehow and
make out the pattern, but not just now.
There was a terrifying word haunting him at

the moment so that he could think of nothing else.

In an amazingly short time he was able to sense the approach of his nurses and helpers ; but the following day puzzled him, for there was a new step, a new voice, and a wonderfully invigorating presence in his room.

" Good morning, Mr. Blake. I've brought my colleague, Doctor Cumming, to see you this morning. How are you ? " It was the voice of the lady doctor.

" You're looking very well," said the new voice. " You'll soon be all right now. We must get rid of this noble swelling over your eyes."

He had not laid a hand on the patient, but Blake was instantly conscious of a feeling of being bucked up. Like grey ghosts at cock-crow the fears which had been haunting him fled.

" Pull up the blind, Doctor, will you ? " said the newcomer. " Now then, not too much." His hands were busy with the band-ages. Blake blinked . . . and shut his eyes again.

" Just shade his right eye while I examine his left," Dr. Cumming said, busily arranging all sorts of complicated-looking apparatus.

"Now look, and tell me what do you see?"

There was a long pause, then Blake spoke.

"I see a grey patch."

"Good! It's the window. Well done! Now the other eye. . . . A little more light, please, Doctor."

They spoke together the technical jargon of their profession, and then Dr. Cumming said: "It's worth trying. Can you stand a little bit of pain?"

"Certainly, Doctor."

"These drops—rather powerful—now then, open your eye . . . shut it now. Painful? It'll be over in a minute."

It was a breathless ordeal, the room was full of the currents and cross-currents of prayer as the two doctors bent over their patient.

"Now then . . . open this eye . . . look!"

There was an age-long pause. "Well, what do you see?" Robert Blake laughed, it had rather a shaky sound, and then he said: "I — I — see — the — face — of— the — girl — who— once— made— me— drink— treacle —beer."

"Thank God!" murmured Elspet Mac-Leod, whose other name was Dr. MacLeod,

D 2

and who could put half the alphabet after her name.

Laughter, perilously near to tears, shook her. Starry-eyed and bright-faced, she sat down suddenly on the side of the patient's bed, which every doctor would tell you is most unprofessional.

Lady MacPherson, who had been hovering on the landing, on hearing happy sounds, entered the bedroom timidly.

"It's all right, Lady MacPherson. The sight is quite back to his right eye and is coming back to his left. He has given us all a bad fright, and me a long journey from London—all for nothing."

There were tears on Lady MacPherson's kind face as she bent over and kissed Robert Blake on the cheek. "Thank God, laddie," she whispered.

"I do, I do! And then my kind doctors and my friends," he said gratefully. Words out of the Old Book floated through his memory : "Joy cometh in the morning," and for those friends who had stood so bravely by him in the black night he had a heart full of gratitude. If there was more than gratitude in his feelings towards Dr. Elspet MacLeod, who can blame him ?

After they had all gone he lay with his eyes closed, thankful and happy. His hands were outside the bed cover and his wandering fingers encountered something that felt like a leaf. He felt it with his other hand. It was a bunch of red rowans.

CHAPTER SIX

HECTOR MacAULAY

Doctor Elspet MacLeod, looking very business-like in her well-cut tweeds and carrying a small leather bag, was hurrying along the road to keep her appointment with Dr. Burgess in Hector MacAulay's house.

The whirr of the reaper machine came from the Home Farm, and, in the crofts, men with scythes were dealing with their crops of oats. But in Hector's corn-patch no attempt had been made to gather in the harvest.

The whole place wore a neglected air which depressed all who saw it. The gate leading into the cornfield had once been the end of an iron bed. Now, tied inadequately to a post with a piece of string, it did little to keep out marauding animals ; in fact, even then, Rosie, Hector's cow, was standing knee-deep in the corn and regarding the world with mild interest.

The little garden in front of the house was in the possession of the hens, and just at that moment they were busily scratching holes among the cabbages. Elspet " shoo'd " them away, to their great indignation.

Hector's wife, Lexie, hearing the cackling of the poultry, came hurrying out to meet her visitor.

" *Beannich mise !* " [1] she exclaimed, with a bright smile. "And is it yourself, *m'eudail?* [2] Myself never can get used to the idea that a doctor can be a real lady. In my young days every doctor of them had his whiskers and his elastic-sided boots and his dog-cart."

Clearly she thought the present-day doctors were sadly lacking.

" Be coming in," she cried hospitably. " Down, Glen—down," to a boisterous collie who was making friendly overtures to the doctor.

" I have Hector in the ben-end," the old woman went on, leading the way. " But he's not liking it at all, at all ! The kitchen is cheerier, he says." She sighed. She was a thin little scrap of a woman with eager bright eyes and a nose and chin which were on friendly terms.

" Not a tooth have I in my head, my dear," she confided to Elspet. " And Hector's the same, and that's the reason I'm not buying beef from the butcher's van ! " And Elspet,

[1] Bless me !
[2] My dear one.

who knew the real reason—which was lack of money—nodded understandingly.

" I'm that thankful I have my good cow," Lexie went on. " She's my greatest help."

" She's eating the corn just now," Elspet said. " Shouldn't I drive her out to the hill ? "

" Not at all, not at all," Lexie cried shrilly. " Rosie's worth a mouthful of corn—see how good she is to me ! And the calf she had the year was a beauty. Three pounds I got for her and that paid the rent."

Even so, Elspet thought it was a mistake to have the corn destroyed. But Lexie had her own views on the matter. " The Lord did not bless me with bairns, but it's as sure as death I'm liking Rosie as well as if I was her mother. And when I'm singing to her she's letting down her milk the bonniest you ever saw."

" Hector," she called. " Here's the lady doctor come to see you. You'll be minding of the little lassie, Elspet MacLeod, who used to be coming here for holidays and staying with her Auntie Eppie at Lochside ? Well, you'd scarcely believe it, but she's turned into a doctor and she's come to see what can be done about your eyes, Hector."

Hector was sitting up in the box-bed, a scarlet nightcap upon his head and his poor, sightless eyes staring straight in front of him. He had the sallow skin of one who is much indoors, and there was about him the look of a chained eagle who is straining desperately at his fetters. A fierce old man, girding at the fate that condemned him to this prison-house of darkness; ready oft-times to "curse God and die."

He stretched out a thin hand gropingly and Elspet took it in her strong clasp. " I mind you fine," he said. " Wasn't it myself that made for you your first fishing rod out of a young rowan tree ? "

" So it was," Elspet laughed. " I can remember yet how beautifully it would bend but never break, and how I was sure I was to catch a twenty-pounder with it some day."

Hector smiled and next minute he gave an impatient sigh. " I have not seen the river for years. Think you, lass, you can do anything for these blind eyes of mine ? "

" There's the other doctor," Lexie announced, as the sound of a motor-car was heard. " Doctor Burgess is coming too, Hector. It's what's called a ' consolation meeting ' they're having about you and is it not proud you should be ? " Lexie was by no means sure how her husband was to submit to this " consolation."

" Well, where are you all ? " a loud voice demanded at the door. " Oh, you've taken my advice and moved MacAulay into the room." Dr. Burgess had entered by this time bringing with him a certain jarring note hard to define but easy to feel.

" Good day, Doctor MacLeod. Nice weather, isn't it ? Did you walk ? A fair long walk from Lochside to Drumcraig."

Before greeting the old folk or giving them a kindly word he stood in the middle of the floor and cast an appraising look around him. Often in out-of-the-way cottages he had picked up a valuable piece of old pottery or pewter ; sometimes he had stumbled on wonderful old pieces of furniture, and once he had secured a carved spinning wheel well-nigh priceless. He found that patients faced by his prompt bill parted with old family treasures (almost) thankfully, in payment of his accounts.

But there was nothing worth taking in Hector's shabby little room. A framed picture of Queen Victoria gazed at him from the mantelpiece and was flanked by great bunches of artificial grasses.

Having satisfied himself that there were no treasures, he turned to the box-bed.

"Now then, MacAulay," he said, "Doctor MacLeod and myself will do our best for you though we don't profess to work miracles. Lexie has promised to see us paid, you understand, even if we don't manage to restore your eyesight."

He was busily taking instruments out of his bag as he talked. "You're an old man, you know, MacAulay, and you can't expect at your age to have all your faculties. How old are you?"

"Seventy-five, sir."

"Now, MacAulay, you can't *always* be seventy-five! You said that the last time I asked you."

Lexie broke in eagerly. "Hector is not the one to say one thing to-day and another to-morrow. When he says a thing he *sticks* to it." She was a loyal if a misguided wife!

Dr. Burgess laughed grimly and Elspet put out her hand and patted the poor hand lying outside Hector's bed cover. She had noticed how it was trembling, and could sense the pain of the old man. Couldn't Dr. Burgess be a little more friendly and human?

"Now, Lexie, be off," Dr. Burgess said

in bullying tones. " We'll let you know all about it presently. I haven't too much time," looking at his watch. " Sit forward, MacAulay, and turn your face this way."

Lexie swallowed a lump in her throat ; the slow, unwilling tears of old age were running down her cheeks as she crept out of the room.

" It will be all right. Cheer up," Elspet whispered. " Hector and I will be glad of a cup of tea when we're done. Have you crowdie ? Well now, isn't that good ! I love crowdie."

Crowdie is curdled milk, and when it is mixed with cream and spread on buttered oatcakes it is food for the gods. Lexie, glad of any task which would take her mind off the ordeal through which her husband was passing, hurried away to the little dairy at the back of the house and got busy with a sieve full of crowdie. She did not spare her cream jar either, and by the time she had the kettle boiling she could hear the room door being opened and the two doctors coming out.

They stood in the garden talking earnestly and Lexie could learn little by looking at their faces. Then Dr. Burgess lifted his hard blue eyes and let them rest on Rosie, still standing contentedly chewing the cud.

" *That* will pay," he said meaningly.

" Let me repeat, Doctor Burgess, I make no charge," Elspet said coldly, and with flashing anger in her eyes.

Dr. Burgess hurried away, chuckling as he went. " Seeing you want to look after the case, you may ! "

.   .   .   .

" Now, Lexie," Elspet cried, " we have good news for you—come away in, and let us share it with Hector. The cataract on his eyes can be removed but his eyes aren't quite ready for it yet. You'll both be patient for a little while yet and then——"

In simple, non-technical words she explained to the terrified old couple what exactly was wrong and how it could be put right.

" By Christmas, Hector, I'll be back for a week's holiday and I'll make all arrangements for your eyes to be put right. Doctor Burgess has left your case in my hands."

" I suppose that nowadays lady doctors are just as good as men." Lexie's tones were polite but she was clearly prejudiced against doctors who were ladies. " The eye is so precious," she said, " and so easily hurt. Will you be giving him the *coloform* ? "

Somewhat ruefully Elspet assured her that lady doctors did their best and that Hector would not get chloroform.

She did not care to tell the old folks that Dr. Burgess declined to take any interest in the case because of the money difficulties.

Hector turned angrily on his wife. " I'm telling you, woman, that it was the lady doctor that examined my eyes and cheered me up, and if the Lord spares me till Christmas I'm going to get my sight back again." He was trembling rather piteously, poor, proud old man.

" Cheers, Hector ! " Elspet said. " You're my second patient. My first is doing well and you're going to do even better. Make Lexie believe that I am a right doctor."

Lexie cried out shrill protestations, and Elspet said she'd forgive her if she brought them all some tea with plenty of cream and sugar and crowdie and oatcakes.

" Thanks to Rosie, I can do that," Lexie said, and while she bustled about in the kitchen Elspet sat talking quietly to the old man. Her voice was a singularly soothing one—that excellent thing in women—and as she talked she could see Hector's quivering nerves growing steady again. And she talked of . . . books ! The books Hector loved, the books she loved, and there was one she knew and loved almost as much as he. It was Bunyan's *Holy War*.

" It's yonder in the kitchen and in the Gaelic," Hector told her. " Many's the time I used to be reading it."

" You'll soon be reading it again. I'm going to bring a book I love and read a chapter to you," Elspet went on. " It's called the *Romance of War*."

" Does it tell of one John Cameron— Colonel John Cameron of Fassiefern ? " he asked eagerly.

" It does."

Hector swallowed. " It's—it's—a book I have been waiting to read for years. I read it when I was a soldier in the Boer War, and now——" he ended with a sigh.

" Now, Hector," she cried briskly, " if you speak like that I'll begin to think I was mistaken when I was calling you a hero."

" Wass you calling me a hero ? " he asked wistfully.

" Indeed I was ; you stood that examination like a—like a—Highland gentleman."

He smiled and there is nothing more touching than the smile of a blind person.

63

Used as Elspet was to the sight of misery, there was something in this humble home that touched her to the heart. Here she was not Dr. Elspet MacLeod, the eye specialist. She was only Elspet, the lass who had known the Glen folk all her days and who shared their joys and sorrow.

Lexie entered with a clattering tray, and the family Bible which had occupied the place of honour on the table was removed and the tea tray put in its place. Glen, the collie, and Morag, the cat, invited themselves to the meal, and an inquisitive hen, after giving them side glances from her bright black eyes, also decided to be present.

It was a merry little meal, though Hector said they should have begun with a dram and Elspet said " not at all "—she wanted tea. And never in her life had she tasted such crowdie.

" I suppose that Sassenach bodies never see anything like it ? " Lexie asked, in gratified tones.

" *Never !* " Elspet's voice was most emphatic, also when Lexie's eye was off her, she took the opportunity to remove a long grey hair which had strayed into the crowdie ! Of such stuff are heroes made !

Lexie and Glen convoyed her part of her way home, and a thankful, relieved old woman was Lexie. She showed to Elspet the other side of a character popularly supposed to be " through-other " and shiftless.

It was a tale of brave endurance which touched her hearer's heart so that she could not say a word.

" There were times I was glad Hector was not seeing so well," Lexie ended up. " What with the land so neglected and the tatties gone with disease it would have broken his heart. The only thing that was keeping me up was Rosie. My blessings on her."

Elspet made a mental note of the fact that there were at least half a dozen young men known to her who must be told about this matter. A few scythes wielded by lusty young arms would secure Lexie's crop. Yes, she must see about it.

CHAPTER SEVEN

THE ROMANCE OF WAR

THE weather had given up pretending it was summer. A keen wind blew down the Glen and sent the withered leaves whirling before it. The bracken no longer looked brave and bronze; it had become seared and grey-looking. The hills had wrapped misty scarves around their shoulders and every burn brawled angrily—so did the river. A dreary world!

Elspet's mood was in keeping with the day, stormy, troubled, and depressed. She was on her way to read to Hector. The following week would see her returning to her duties in the London hospital. She was glad her work remained, she told herself, and stifled a sigh that rose to her lips.

"Work and time cure all troubles," she told herself sternly. "The happiest women are the single ones, who have time to give themselves to their work and to help the world a little."

"The depression over Iceland" had set in the previous afternoon during her visit to Orrin Lodge. Robert Blake had gone out for a walk, Lady MacPherson explained with many apologies. " I persuaded him to go for Alice's sake," she went on. " The child has simply sat for hours by his side reading the driest stuff ever written—statistics and reports and things ! All in connection with his work, of course, and of vital importance to him, but to Alice they must have been boring beyond words ! She reads till she's hoarse, and though she doesn't say a word, I'm *sure* she suffers a lot of pain in that hurt hand of hers. You know it's still in a sling. Ah, well," Lady MacPherson smiled as at some happy secret thought, " I'm hoping that dear Alice, who is the daughter of an old school friend of mine and in whose welfare I have a warm interest, will have no need to be anxious about *her* future after this." She nodded knowingly and added : " I've been quite interested in ' Love's young dream.' "

Elspet was pondering over this matter now. There was only one deduction to be drawn, and Elspet drew it, and her heart ached with a pain that was physical.

Resolutely she turned her thoughts towards the old folk at Drumcraig. Hector proved himself to be a regular fire-eater and had gloried in all the warlike chapters of the book.

When they came to the death of Colonel John Cameron, at Quatre Bras, Hector turned his face to the wall. " I'm hearing the pipes," he murmured, " and they're playing *Oran au Aiog*, the death song of the Clan."

They had reached the last chapter in the book. Lexie, her spectacles balanced on the very end of her nose, had undertaken to read a chapter occasionally when Hector wished his memory refreshed. Elspet was not needed now. Every woman loves to think she is needed particularly by one person. Elspet had imagined her other patient had needed her. Well, he had not. " Alice Miles——"

She choked over the name. " At any rate my patients in hospital need me." She squared her shoulders and held her head high. She was wearing for the first time her new brogues fashioned for her by Dennis O'Brian, a little old Irish shoemaker who had drifted into the Glen years ago. He must have been *sib* to the Leprecaun and have learnt from one of that goblin race the cunning art of brogue-making. He loved to make Elspet's brogues because her feet were worthy of his best work, he used to say. " And her walking yonder like a mountain roe among the heather."

She now put her best foot foremost, and,

68

at the bend of the road, as she swung along she went bang into a woman leading a cow and followed by a dejected-looking dog.

" Lexie," she gasped in amazement, " where are you and Rosie going ? " Lexie regarded her coldly. " It's a nice day, Miss—I mean Doctor MacLeod," she said with awful chill politeness.

" It is *not* a nice day, Lexie, and don't you pretend it," Elspet said, " and you haven't told me why you're all taking a walk. Now, Glen, don't try to eat my new shoes."

She could see that Lexie had been weeping bitterly, and a queer fear awoke in her heart. " Tell me at once where you are going," she said sternly.

" I'm going—to—to—sell my cow."

" Sell Rosie ! "

Lexie burst into tears and threw her arms round Rosie's neck, much to that animal's astonishment.

" They're telling me that Sandy Morrison, the merchant, is looking for a cow that is a good milker, and I'm going to him with Rosie."

There was some mystery here. " How is Hector ? " Elspet asked.

" He's fine, and six nor seven lads came the other night and cut our corn."

" Is that why you are selling Rosie ? "
Elspet laughed.

Lexie looked angrily at her. " You're not
needing to ask me, are you ? " she said bitterly.
" After you and Doctor Burgess sending me
this letter."

She drew out of her bosom a paper, soiled
with much handling and stained with tears.
It was a bill from Dr. Burgess " for professional
service and for the consultation with Dr. E.
MacLeod, Oculist, of London," and the
amount was for ten guineas.

" He said," Lexie went on dully, " that
if we had not the money we could just be
selling Rosie and because I was determined
to have the ' consolation ' I must pay for it,
and at once, too."

" He ? Doctor Burgess, I suppose ? "
Lexie nodded.

" I'll take charge of this letter, if you please,
Lexie. Meanwhile, you and Rosie and Glen
will please go home. You've had a nice walk.
You'll be tired if you go any farther. Tell
Hector I'll be along before I go back to work.
Meantime I must hurry home. I have a letter
to write."

Her eyes were blazing, the red flags of
danger were flying in her cheeks. She looked,

Lexie said, " awesome bonnie." All the same it was well for Dr. Charles Burgess that he did not meet her just then, for the fighting blood of her clan was racing through her veins and pounding in her temples.

Lexie, with a face in which sunshine and shadow were strangely interwoven, watched the hurrying figure as it disappeared along the road. " The blessings of the Benign Being be on her," she murmured, falling back on an old and a pagan blessing of the Gael. " Now, I know what the good Book means when it says : ' How beautiful are the feet of them that bring good tidings.' "

" The Lord is good," old Hector said, after Lexie had told him her joyous news.

" He's lavish," Lexie replied, in a perfect passion of gratitude, putting two cold potatoes to roast in front of the peat fire.

CHAPTER EIGHT

CRANBERRY JAM

THE day so full of disagreeable things had merged into a night equally unpleasant. Rain fell with deadly persistency, and, when Elspet announced that she was going to the post office, Aunt Eppie begged her to wait till the morning.

" And lose the post ? " she asked. " I don't mind the wind and the rain—in fact, to-night, I feel I'd rather enjoy them. No, MacDougall, I don't think I'll take you." This to the dog, who had offered her his escort.

Her aunt turned to her work, which was the making of cranberry jam. There is no task which more delights the heart of a woman than this one of jam- and jelly-making, and Aunt Eppie's face wore a contented look as she moved about from the jelly-pan, swung over the fire, to the table with its array of empty jars.

A basket full of crab apples and rowan berries, which were presently to follow the cranberries, made a colourful note on the old kitchen dresser.

The glowing red peats gave you welcome, and MacDougall, the young cocker spaniel did the same. He was horribly in Aunt Eppie's way, but when she said so he just rolled on his back and offered his tummy to be tickled. Failing that he offered to lay his muddy paws and wet body on the "resting chair." West and East met in this chair, for the wood of which it was made had been grown in the Glen and fashioned by John-the-Joiner. The gay cushions and blanket that covered its angular frame had come from the East, and had all its gorgeous colours, a piece of extravagance for which Elspet was responsible. And did MacDougall really think he was to lie there?

The floor was covered with deer skins, and the dog was offered one of these. An ancient grandfather clock which rumbled and chuckled before announcing the hour, did what it liked with time. It was something like Captain Cuttle's watch which, " if you put it back half an hour every morning and another quarter of an hour towards the afternoon, was a watch that would do you credit." The cheap but reliable alarum clock on the mantelpiece regarded its colleague with cold contempt.

Aunt Eppie glanced at its pert white face.

" Twenty-five minutes brisk boiling," she murmured, consulting the cookery book. " I wonder can I dish it ? "

She examined a saucer in the window where she had put a spoonful of jelly to " jell," and decided it would do ; longer boiling might spoil the lovely colour.

She swung the jelly-pan on to the table and began filling the jars when a brisk rap came to the kitchen door.

" Come in," she cried, without lifting her eyes from her work.

" Good evening, Miss MacLeod. Is the doctor to be seen ? "

She looked up then. " I beg your pardon, Sir Donald. I thought it was some witless bairn with a penny burning a hole in his pocket."

" There's no penny burning a hole in my pocket, but there's a half-remembered tune dancing through my head that's annoying me. I can't get it right ! And Elspet promised she'd help me."

Aunt Eppie then saw he was carrying a fiddle case beneath his dripping mackintosh.

" She's away to the post office with a letter she had to write in a great hurry," Aunt Eppie explained. " Take off your wet coat and come in and sit down, if you please. Myself, I'm at the jam-making here."

"And doesn't it smell good?" he said. "Cranberries? Are they plentiful this year?"

"Yes, if you know where to look," she replied, with a twinkle in her eye. Then she added apropos of nothing in particular: "I'm sure the Lord never meant the grouse to get *all* the berries, whatever the Laird may say."

MacDougall, who was making his usual friendly overtures, thought he might take a bite out of Sir Donald's sporran. They were arguing the matter when Elspet returned.

The writing of that letter to Dr. Burgess had been a satisfactory piece of work. She had written such blistering words, the marvel was the writing paper didn't catch fire! And she was feeling ever so much better! "Fighting with wild beasts," brings a certain amount of satisfaction if you win the fight.

The wind had whipped the fresh colour into her cheeks; the rain had made her hair curl all round her ears, and anger had made her eyes bright. In her tweed coat and suede hat with its pheasant's wing she made an attractive picture as she stood beneath Aunt Eppie's hanging lamp.

" What are *you* doing in our kitchen ? " she demanded of Sir Donald.

"I was invited to come in," he replied. "Your aunt asked me ! I defy you to put me out ! "

She laughed gaily. After all, it was good to be young and alive and have a job of work, even if it included the teaching of Gaelic songs to this young Celt. She had once thought that she would have the teaching of the Gaelic language to Robert Blake. A mistake !

" Fourteen pounds," Aunt Eppie announced triumphantly. " Besides two breakfast-cup-fuls." She referred to her jelly.

" I propose we sample the breakfast-cup-fuls," Sir Donald said.

" Dare—just you dare ! " cried Elspet, hurrying to help her aunt to carry the jars to the cold pantry.

When she returned she was carrying her clarsach and a bundle of music.

" Aunt Eppie had a customer in the shop the other day, one of the young ladies from Orrin Lodge, and she told Auntie that if I had my voice trained I might in time be quite a nice singer ! I couldn't help wondering what old Hamish MacGregor who taught me so carefully would have said if he had heard her." She laughed gleefully.

" Was it that tall, fair girl who looked at us all as if we were specimens from the Zoo ? " he asked. " I'm sure she refers to us as ' natives ' and marvels we aren't still wearing skins and forgetting to do our hair," quoth Sir Donald. Then he added : " *Those English !* "

" There are some quite nice English people," Elspet said, wishing to be fair to everyone.

" Perhaps," he admitted with reluctance. " Where's the music of the ' Boat Song ' ? "

Then the talk became entirely technical. She sounded chords on the clarsach and kept on sounding them until his fiddle responded to the challenge truly and musically.

" Now for the rhythm," she said. " Remember they were carrying their Chief to his burial place in Iona and sadness was on them."

A slow, mournful note wailed through the kitchen, then an even slower one. It was too much for MacDougall ; he howled dismally and refused to be comforted, so Aunt Eppie shut him up in the shop.

She also swung on the kettle and set the brown teapot to warm on a hot peat. A cup of tea was called for after all the sadness. The musicians were too engrossed in their task to spare a thought for anything else. Elspet was

humming the tune and Sir Donald was adding
a harmonious bass when, for the second time
in this evening, there was a tap at the kitchen
door.

" I wonder may I have some cigarettes,
please ? " Elspet was the first to recognise
the voice, and with a startled air she sprang
to her feet. " Mr. Blake, we are so sorry !
We have been making so much noise that even
if the last trump had sounded or MacDougall
had howled we wouldn't have heard."

" Please carry on," he said pleasantly.
" MacDougall has already told me what he
thinks about your music, but I am sure that
in time one might get used to it—one might
even like it ! No, I'm not wet, the rain is
over."

Elspet and Sir Donald exchanged horrified
glances. " Did anyone speak about pearls
before swine ? " Elspet murmured.

" Or the clarsach before a Sassenach ? " Sir
Donald added.

" I am not a Sassenach," Robert Blake pro-
tested. " I have told you my mother was a
Scot—a Robertson—in fact my proper name is
Robertson Blake."

" Hear to that now," Aunt Eppie said
amiably. " And how are you feeling, sir, after

that bad accident, and how is the young lady ? "

" Fine, thank you. Miss Miles is all right, too. By rights I should be back at work, but I have got an extension of leave from an indulgent government."

" That explains our present high taxation," Elspet said wrathfully. " I won't pay any more income-tax ! "

Then the talk became general. The shooting season was to end, as usual, with a dance called the " Ghillies' Ball," though everyone who could, attended it.

This year Lady MacPherson had decreed that the first part of the entertainment would be a fancy dress affair for the young folk, with prizes for the most ingenious dress, and masks for everyone.

This led to much anxious thought among the young folk, and to much injured feeling on the part of Rob, the cattleman. Sir Donald told the story with great gusto. Rob had consulted his friend, Tom MacKay, as to a suitable disguise. Now Rob was easily the dirtiest man in the Glen. " Wash your face, Rob, and put on a clean shirt," Tom had advised him. " And I'm telling you not a creature will know who you are."

" I shall disguise myself as a lady," Elspet declared. " Old Lexie MacAulay can't believe that a doctor can be a ' leddy.' I'd like to prove to her and to all the other Glen folks that she can be both."

" I'll testify to your skill as a doctor," Blake laughed, " whether you administer beer (treacle or herb) or restore one's eyes."

" Then, I'm afraid there's no use my aspiring to be a ' real leddy.' Well, well, I have a good mind to go to the Ghillies' Ball dressed as a gipsy."

" Do," urged both her hearers, and Robert Blake added : " Wear a knot of red rowans so that we'll know you." He looked at her, and the " love licht was in his e'ee " as he spoke.

" Not so fast, my good patient," she cried, and tried to still the joyous up-leap of her heart, " though it's an old belief that if a woman wears a knot of red rowans in her bodice or girdle she is safe from bewitchment and the evil eye."

" But who would wish to put the evil eye on you ? " he asked smiling, and when Robert Blake smiled he did it with his eyes, and so she simply *had* to like him. She realised then that he was really quite young and presumably a little daft and that he was ready to be on terms of friendliness or even of something warmer !

The knowledge sent a blush to her face, and caused her to look intently into the fire as if she saw something gladsome in its red lowes.[1] Into her voice came a sweetness, a softness, an intoxicating tone of confidence and intimacy. She glanced at him shyly as if he were an unfamiliar person or rather a familiar person in an unfamiliar setting.

" And what are you to wear at the fancy dress ball ? " she asked Sir Donald with, as it were, a gay farewell wave to the pictures in the fire.

" I intend going as the Loch Ness Monster, complete with cocked bonnet and bagpipes," he replied solemnly.

" And humps ? "

" No, two friends have promised to be my humps and hind legs. We're having a practice to see that we can all ' galumph ' properly and at the same time. It would be disastrous if the front legs had to tell the hind ones ' it's your turn now.' "

" I thought of going as Prince Charlie," Robert Blake said in a tentative voice.

" Far too obvious," Elspet cried. " There

---

[1] Flames.

will be dozens of ' Prince Charlies,' just as there will be dozens of ' Queen Maries.' "

" I can't think of anything more original."

" And you a Robertson of Struan ? What about your great ancestor Donnachadh Reambar, chief of your clan, who fought at Bannockburn ? Why, it is said that before the battle he found a magic stone—called the ' banner stone,' which gave the Scots their victory that day."

" I never heard of him," he confessed.

" You're a disgrace to your clan," she retorted. " Such ignorance is enough to make old Donnachadh turn in his grave. If you *must* go as Prince Charlie please wear something by which we will know you."

" Yes, do," Sir Donald said wickedly. " Put your sporran round your neck or your kilt back to the front."

" And make our bonnie Prince turn in *his* grave next," Elspet stormed. " Wear a knot of red ribbon to fasten your hair. That's as lucky as red rowans. ' Rowan tree and red threid send the witches on their speed.' "

Before anyone could reply MacDougall lifted up his voice in a series of angry barks. " I'm shut up in the shop," he complained, " and someone is slipping from door to door listening at the keyhole and peering through the window. Why don't you take some notice of me ? "

Aunt Eppie laid down her teapot. . . . There was no one there. . . . She looked out of the door. Along the road in the direction of Orrin Lodge the tail light of a bicycle was disappearing in the darkness.

CHAPTER NINE

THE GHILLIES' BALL

In Highland places the date for any festivity is always arranged with reference to the moon ; not, be it noted, for any superstitious reason, but simply because of the light.

On the night of the Ghillies' Ball the October moon filled the Glen with silver radiance. The village hall looked like something out of fairyland with its strings of coloured lanterns, festooned over the rustic porch and round the windows.

Pipers and fiddlers were tuning up their instruments, there was the promise of much gaiety in the air.

All sorts of vehicles, from push bikes to luxurious saloon cars, were bringing the guests, and Hamish Stewart who was acting as "M.C." tried to solve the problem of being not in two places, but in half a dozen at the same moment.

Never had the moon looked down on such a strange company in Glen Orrin ! Pirates and Red Indians rubbed shoulders with fierce-looking Highlanders. "Flora MacDonald" and "Cinderella" whispered secrets to each other, while hikers and Arab sheikhs exchanged cigarettes and jokes.

Sir Hugh and Lady MacPherson received their strange-looking guests with words of gracious welcome. "To judge the fancy dresses is going to be a difficult business," Lady MacPherson said, looking after a weird-looking object, or was it a number of weird-looking objects? It evidently possessed six legs and four humps and it came "galumph-ing" in. Undoubtedly the "Loch Ness Monster."

And now she had to greet a young "gipsy," a picturesque figure with a leaf-brown cloak over her shoulders and its red-lined hood pulled over her head. She had a bodice of the same colour laced over a white under-blouse. In the lacings she had tucked a bunch of rowan berries, and from her ears hung great silver rings. Gay glass bracelets dangled from her wrists. Her black velvet mask gave no hint as to her identity, though one at least of her fellow dancers told himself he knew who she was.

He himself was "Prince Charlie" at his most splendid moment, with his golden wig curled and tied with a broad red ribbon. "Long John Silver," "Capt'n Flint" upon his shoulder, came tap, tapping after him, his air as sinister as ever.

" Partners for the ' Grand March,' " shouted the " M.C.," and Dugald MacRae, head gamekeeper, came up and with a bow presented his arm to Lady MacPherson. The Laird did the same to the keeper's wife and everyone else followed suit. The pipes skirled, the drones roared, the dancers cried " hooch " and with snapping of fingers and whirling of kilts and frocks, the " Grand March " merged into the " Reel of Tulloch."

The amount of energy a Highlander puts into a reel is amazing. The floor of the hall swung beneath dancing feet ; the rafters rung with the music. Robert Blake felt the blood of his forefolk dancing through his veins as he swung his partner through all the figures of the reel. He had never lived till this evening— and now, and now ! Life was an unimagined gaiety, the touch of his partner's hand, the feel of her body as he put his arms round her intoxicated him.

" There's a moon to-night," he whispered. " I have something I should like to say to you by the light of the moon."

She nodded, the red rowans in her bosom trembled.

" You won't be cold ? " he asked anxiously
and then because he was akin to the immortals,
he said : " My plaidie to the angry airt I'd
shelter thee, I'd shelter thee." Incomparable
song of all lovers ! . . .

" At the porch, then, at ten o'clock," he
whispered. " I don't see how I'm to wait so
long ! Lady MacPherson said I must dance
duty dances—I don't dance duty dances with
you, my gipsy maid," he said, his lips brushing
the top of her head—and then the music
ceased.

.   .   .   .   .

The loch was like a sheet of polished silver
and the fir trees put their heads close together
and whispered as " Prince Charlie " and " the
gipsy maid " walked slowly along beneath the
light of the moon.

" What does he say ? " asked the trees.
Though they had seen many lovers they had
never lost their interest in them.

They could hear the man's voice murmuring
—they nudged each other and listened atten-
tively for the other voice—the voice of " the
gipsy maid," but she gave her answer without
words and the " Prince " drew her into his arms
and kissed her soft white chin. He was con-

scious, he knew not why, of a feeling of vague disappointment. "Take off the mask," he said, and tried to pull it away. But she whispered "No" and fled swift as a deer back to the hall.

The Laird and his lady, with Kirsty Campbell as "casting voter," stood on the platform. The "M.C." sent the mummers in couples to parade round the hall. "Prince Charlie" found himself escorting a Celtic bardess in her strange symbolic robes. His gipsy maid, he noted with annoyance, was in the care of "Long John Silver." The "Monster," who must have been a Mormon, had three ladies in his care. He explained that he wanted a wife "good, wise and beautiful," and this could only be managed by marrying the three ladies.

CHAPTER TEN

"MELODION NANNIE"

No one had noticed a strange, tattered-looking creature who had slipped quietly in. Now she had taken her place at the end of the row. "Melodion Nannie" everyone thought, and wondered how the door-keeper had let in this extremely unpleasant tramp, who for a copper would dance and play weird tunes on her ancient melodion.

Her feet were thrust into boots several sizes too big for her so that she shuffled along clumsily; her striped petticoat was tattered, a weather-beaten shawl was crossed over her shoulders and knotted behind; under one arm she carried her melodion; over the other was slung a tin pail with several smaller ones inside, including her own tea pail, black with smoke. On her head was perched an old felt hat several sizes too small, and her straggling black hair hung down untidily over her face and neck. In the corner of her mouth was an ancient black pipe. A black stocking out of which two holes had been cut, covered the upper part of her face, and from behind this her eyes peered brightly. Round her neck hung a long string of red rowans.

" It's ' Melodion Nannie,' " Mrs. MacLean, the keeper's wife, whispered to her husband. " That's our Nellie's old hat. I gave it to her a year ago. She's drunk, I believe."

" Well, Nannie," the Laird called out, " we all know you. Come along and give us a song and a dance."

The company cheered the suggestion ; it was a " daft ploy," but to-night was the night for daftness ; to-morrow, winter and gloom would settle on the Glen.

Nannie shook her untidy head, but eager hands pushed the poor creature into the middle of the floor. " A song, Nannie, give us a song," they cried. " We'll have a collection afterwards."

Her struggles ceased when she heard this. Lady MacPherson was displeased with her husband. " She'll just spend the money in drink," she told him, but he was quite unrepentant. " Come on, Nannie," he shouted, and she shambled into the space cleared for her.

She laid down the tin pail—and taking the melodion between her two dirty hands and with an awkward bow she broke into a curious ranting song. "Can you wash a sailor's shirt, can you wash it clean?" she inquired.

Then she broke into a second song. She had laid aside her melodion and with only one big pail slung over her arm she sang "The Lilt of the Potato Gatherers." In a moment she had transported the company to the potato fields and they were all bending over the upturned furrows and throwing the potatoes into pails. It was communal labour with plenty of cheery laughter, and what was to hinder the gatherers, when they reached the end of their drill and their pails were full, from dancing a few steps?

Nannie kicked off her clumsy boots and as light as a feather she was dancing at the end of the row, hands on hips and the heaped-up potato pail beside her. The company could see it all; it was work in which they had all engaged. They could see, too, the ill-natured *boddach* approaching Nannie and scolding her, and how they laughed when Nannie retaliated by dancing gaily up to his full pail and with a kick sent the potatoes flying "helter skelter!"

"Prince Charlie" had watched the per-

formance with mixed feelings. Who was
"Melodion Nannie"? He was conscious of a
queer sinking in his heart. The girl who danced
with such gay abandon was no wandering
tramp. Then, who, *who*, was the gipsy maid
who had plighted her troth with him? Dully
he remembered thinking that "the gipsy lass"
did not seem so tall as usual, neither had he
felt the thrill he had expected, but possibly
her strange dress would account for this.
True, she had refused to take off her mask.
Had Fate and the moonlight played a cruel
trick upon him?

He heard his name called out as a prize-
winner and was told to remove his mask.
"All masks off," the Laird commanded.

Like a man in a dream, Robert Blake looked
about him surprised, yet not so surprised either,
to find Alice Miles smiling sweetly into his
face.

"I've told Lady MacPherson," she murmured, "and she's coming to congratulate
us when the prize-giving is over. Aren't the
tricks of Fate strange?" she went on, in her
sweet voice.

"Melodion Nannie" was shuffling up to
receive her prize and to reveal her identity.

"The best disguise in the hall," Lady

MacPherson said, and handed Elspet her prize
—a string of crimson coral beads.

"Thank you very much," said Elspet. "I've
broken my own string. It doesn't matter. It
was only made of red rowans."

CHAPTER ELEVEN

BURIED TREASURE

Elspet MacLeod was digging a hole in the bottom of her aunt's garden. So absorbed was she in her task, she gave a nervous start when she heard her name called out.

With her right foot still on the spade, she straightened her back and looked towards the speaker.

" I'm so sorry," she said apologetically. " I never saw you."

" I know," Kirsty Campbell agreed ruefully. " You were working with such deadly concentration and energy I concluded you were digging the grave of your dearest enemy. I haven't seen you since the night of the Ghillies' Ball when you baffled us all by your likeness to ' Melodion Nannie.' Are you burying her to-day ? "

" No," Elspet said, raising her eyes from her spade and Kirsty was struck by the thinness of her face and the restlessness of her eyes. " I'm burying . . . summer ! "

" Without benefit of clergy ? "

" Yes."

" Where's the corpse ? "

" There, in that old biscuit-box."

Kirsty looked puzzled. " I'm burying rowans," Elspet said, " and at Christmas I intend to resurrect them. If they are the rowans I take them to be they'll be as red and fresh as ever."

" I must try that plan, too," Kirsty said thoughtfully. " We have plenty of rowans in Lochaber, but we just allow the birds to eat them."

" Square matters by giving the birds some corn, and if you've no holly berries at Christmas you'll find the rowans coming in very handily."

" I'm going home to-morrow," Kirsty said, " and the moment I get there I'll dig a grave, too." Then with seeming irrelevance she said : " Jock MacKintosh went away this morning. He has to join his regiment at once. They're going to Egypt."

The eyes of both girls met with a world of mutual understanding.

" He *is* a nice boy," Elspet said in her warmest voice.

" Yes, he is, and he thought me a nice girl

till dear Alice Miles showed him his mistake," Kirsty said bitterly.

"Is—is—*she* a nice girl?" Elspet asked.

"Oh, very—a sweet girl. She should be called 'Alice Smiles' instead of 'Alice Miles'! She's the sort of girl that says in her sweet way 'Come along now, girls, let's all sit round the fire and talk about our boy friends.' But if she had made up her mind that she was going to steal your boy friend, you don't need to think anything would stop her." Kirsty laughed again, but there was no mirth in her laughter. "You know that, don't you, Elspet?"

Elspet was not the girl to wear her heart on her sleeve, so she kept silent; but the fact that Kirsty had suffered as she had done gave her a strangely friendly feeling to this girl. Kirsty sensed this and asked suddenly: "Do you think this engagement to Robert Blake was engineered by our dear Alice? I know she changed her fancy dress at the last moment. She had meant to go as Diana, the Huntress, then, quite suddenly, she discovered the costume of this heathen goddess was not '*quite nice.*' She must have spent a little fortune in telegrams to London for the gipsy dress. Possibly she thought it was no time to be economical and results have proved that she was right."

Elspet was measuring the hole in the earth, and now fitted the biscuit-box into its grave. " I hope they'll be happy," she said.

" Let's say we hope she'll be as happy as she deserves," Kirsty amended. " If Robert Blake is a happy man he doesn't look it. They departed last night, she very much the blushing bride-to-be and he like a man haunted by a ghost."

Elspet chuckled. " You don't spare your friends, do you ? " she asked.

" Spare your friends, and spoil the crack, my dear girl ! By praising everybody to everybody else your conversation is as exciting as a milk sociable and no one is deceived by it. Let's be frank, I say."

" All right," Elspet replied. " I'm very sorry I did not know about you and Captain Jock. But—but—now that Alice has deserted him, couldn't you——? "

" Whistle him back ? " Kirsty tossed her head. - " You see, I'm not sure it is my pride or my heart that is most hurt. Jock is a dear boy—I liked him fine. We laughed at the same jokes and grew gloomy and Celtic over the same woes. But I'm wondering if that would be enough to go through life with."

Elspet looked at her with a twinkle in her eye. " I think you'll get over it in time," she said. " And I hope——" she paused awkwardly.

" You hope you'll do the same," Kirsty said cheerfully. " Do you know, Elspet, I'm very glad we've had this talk—I'm feeling ever so much better. ' A fellow feeling makes us wondrous kind.' I must be off now to the post office to collect letters and send telegrams. Jessie Melville, the Lodge housemaid, is awfully kind and loans me her bike. Dear Alice, in her sweet way, used it quite a lot and returned it with a punctured tyre after riding it to the village one terrifically cold, wet night. We all thought she had gone to meet Blake, for he was in the village too, but we were wrong. She came back alone and in a very bad temper. It was that very night she changed her mind about the ' Diana ' costume."

Elspet looked up. " I remember that night," she said. " Can you tell me is the marriage to be soon ? "

" Just as soon as Uncle Robert, who is

making young Robert his heir, hurries away to Heaven! I understand he's an invalid, and I'm sure dear Alice will arrange that he departs at a convenient time. I see your grave is finished. R.I.P."

CHAPTER TWELVE

CALLUM

Lochside,
Inverness-shire,
November, 193—

"My Dear Elspet,

"I write you these few lines to let you know I am well except for the rheumatism, and hoping you enjoy the like blessing."

So wrote Aunt Eppie to her niece now back in London. Her writing was as careful as her English ; yet she managed to make the little doings of the Glen very real and very living. The pig had been killed and was of a quite wonderful weight (twenty-one stone without a word of a lie !) and the young hens were laying and wasn't that a blessing ? The game-keeper's wife at the Birches had got twins, and the Glen singing-class had begun, and Colin, the precentor, was that angry at the young folk because they had been asking to learn human hymns instead of the psalm tunes, and the weather was wet and cold so that the old folk were all feeling their years. Lexie, at Drumcraig, had taken to her bed partly through a bad dose of the cold and partly because of grief for her dog that had been killed by the butcher's van. It seemed that Lexie was not in the way of buying beef and the butcher went past her house like lightning !

"I was thinking to myself that if I'm spared till next week and if you've no objections I might give Lexie my last year's knitted jacket, seeing you've sent me another. MacDougall is very well but very wicked, for didn't he eat the feet out of the new stockings you sent me—the rascal ! "

Elspet smiled whimsically as she read her letter (it smelt of peats).

"I must send Auntie another pair of stockings," she thought, and wondered would Aunt Eppie's last year's woollen jacket really comfort Lexie for the death of her well-loved dog. Anyway, the kindly human sympathy that prompted the gift would certainly help.

She gave a little sigh as she replaced the letter in its envelope. For just a twink she had been back in the Glen where, it must be admitted, the gloomy wet weather had its effect upon the folk. Elspet used to declare that it was climate and not Calvin that made the Highlanders so gloomy. But they had their gay moments, too !

She had a heavy day's work before her.

" Eliza," she said to her prim, efficient, but scarcely human housekeeper, " I don't think I'll be late to-night—dinner at seven, please, but I may have to go out afterwards."

Eliza said in her toneless voice : " Very well, Doctor Mac-Le-od, I shall attend to that."

" I wonder," Elspet said to herself as she hurried to catch her bus, " what like Eliza is inside. If I had time I'd dissect her ! I'm sure I'd find neat little gadgets and boxes and clockworks all tidily arranged. She has no guts—not one." From which it will be seen that Elspet was no " real leddy " to speak in such a fashion !

She reminded herself of Eliza's many excellencies—her cooking—her punctuality—the efficient way in which she repaired the doings of a too exuberant laundry. " If only she'd let me be untidy, and if only she'd pronounce my name properly, I'd like her ever so much better," she said.

She had a long, hard day and life seemed a dreary business when at last she left the clinic to return to her flat. Her last case had been that of a young farmer who had surprised a poacher in his field and had got a charge of rabbit shot full in the face. . . . He had come guided by his young wife, an elfin slip of a lass with great eyes several sizes too big for her little, white face. It hadn't been easy to tell this couple the hopelessness of the case . . . that the man would never see again. He had broken down pitifully and said : " You'll not love me any more, Lill." And then that little handful of a wife of his had put her arms round his neck and said : " My dear, a woman loves a man fifty times more when he needs her. I'll be eyes for us both."

Where, Elspet wondered, had this little scrap of a girl got her wisdom, or was it simply what every woman knows ? Somehow her thoughts drifted back to another case when Dr. Cumming had asked a stricken man : " What do you see ? " and he had answered : " I—I—see—the—face—of—a— girl — who — made — me — once — drink — treacle—beer."

She was passing Broadleaf's, in Oxford Street, when she suddenly bethought herself that she'd buy Aunt Eppie a new pair of stockings. She might even buy something gay, but quite useless, to comfort Lexie. What would it be ? " A flannel petticoat," her sensible self suggested. " Certainly not," said her daft self, and she began to explore the fascinating shop. A gift to cheer one should never be something useful !

How she chanced to find her way into the department where pet animals were sold she never knew. As usual, there was a noisy crowd in the place and the atmosphere was stuffy and hot and smelly. She looked in at the door and caught the wistful and almost human eyes of a little monkey sitting in a cage. Poor little scrap—he looked bewildered among the crowd of human beings. Very unwillingly Elspet took another step into the room ; she hated to see these caged creatures, yet she had to satisfy herself that they were not all un-happy.

The Persian kittens in the next cage were gambolling about, flirting openly with their many admirers. They were sure to get good homes, she thought thankfully, and then in the next cage she met the steady gaze of a little Scots terrier.

He was sitting at the back of his cage, and the hurt, desolate look of him brought a queer tightness to her throat.

" *M'eudail*," she murmured, sitting on her heels the better to see him. But he was, like all Scotties, an aloof and dignified gentleman.

" Come, *m'eudail*, and speak to me," she said again. Something in the tones of her voice appealed to the Scottie. Slowly he

advanced towards her. She pushed her hand
through the bars and put it on his hot little
head.

" Darling, you have a headache," she said.

" Wouldn't *you* have a headache if you were
here ? " his reproachful eyes asked.

She stroked him tenderly and he leaned his
head against the cage like a weary, homesick
bairn. He liked this strange person who spoke
to him as no one had ever spoken to him since
his own loved master so mysteriously had left
him in this awful noisy place.

" Take me with you," he urged. " I don't
like this place. There's always lights and
noise, and no one has time to speak to me.
Yes, they feed me, but I'm never hungry."

He looked eagerly into her face. " You're
taking me, aren't you ? " he asked breathlessly. His tail and his ears had been flat and
dejected ; now they were erect and his eyes
were as bright as diamonds.

" But, my dear, I *can't* take you," Elspet said
miserably. " What would I do with a Scottie
in my tiny flat up three flights of stairs and
with no garden for you to run in ? And what
would Eliza say ? "

The Scottie had put his two hairy paws on
her knees. His tail wagged so energetically he

nearly fell, but, " You're taking me," he pleaded.

Elspet suddenly stood erect. " I can't take you," she repeated, and would have said more only she could not. Bitterly she repented having come in at all. She took a step towards the door. " For goodness sake, doggie, don't look at me like that—you make me feel like a —a—worm," she whispered. She hurried away, trying to tell herself that such a nice dog would soon be all right, he'd be sure to find a good home. She was all the time miserably conscious of the pained and surprised eyes of the Scottie following her with dumb reproach.

Irresolute, she stood on the threshold of the door—inclination pulling her one way, common sense the other.

The man in charge came up to her. " That's a thoroughbred Scottie, modom," he told her. " His master had to go abroad in a great hurry and his orders were that the dog was not to be sold unless we were sure he'd get a good home. Otherwise he's to be destroyed. Pity too, for he's a nice little chap. Not every man's dog, of course, but faithful to them as he does take to."

" *Otherwise he's to be destroyed.*" Those

sinister words decided the question, and at the same moment Elspet had a brain-wave . . . she'd buy the Scottie and send it to Lexie MacAulay !

" What's his name ? " she asked.

The man consulted a ledger. " Callum," he answered, " and here's his pedigree," and he produced a formidable-looking document. Evidently Callum's pedigree was equal to that of the lady love of the " Laird o' Cockpen " !

" I'll buy him," she said.

With the mere uttering of these momentous words the gloom and depression and the final acute misery which had been piling up all day suddenly fell, like Pilgrim's burden, from off her shoulders ! Joyfully she retraced her footsteps to the cage where a little, dejected bundle was watching her with miserable eyes.

" *M'eudail*, you're coming with me," she whispered. Perhaps it was the words—perhaps it was the look on her face—one can't tell, but in an instant the Scottie was as joyous and excited as herself.

" He do seem to have taken to you, modom," the keeper said. " I haven't seen that dog with his ears pricked or his tail up since he's been here. He just don't take no notice of anyone."

" Callum," she said, and laughed at his excited response. For five minutes they rejoiced over each other, the world forgetting but *not* by the world forgot, for now that the sale was completed the keeper wished to get rid of customer and dog.

" Shall we send him for you, modom ? "

" No, no, I'll take him," Elspet replied, and tucked Callum beneath her arm. He was a stout little gentleman and objected to be carried, so when they reached the street she let him down. He stood snuffing the fresh air and then he uttered a long " woof " of joy. It told more than any mere words !

It was a case for a taxi, and as Elspet sat with Callum on her lap she rehearsed the forthcoming scene with the horrified Eliza.

" But I don't care for Eliza," Elspet said to Callum—or was it to herself? " If she's not pleased she can just go ! Anyway, it's only till I go home at Christmas. And I won't grovel to my maid." Oh, a lion was nothing to Elspet at that moment !

Once she thought she'd stop the taxi and 'phone to Eliza that she was bringing home a gentleman friend. " It would serve her right," she thought wickedly, " only I can't be bothered." The real reason was that Callum was curled up in her lap, his nose in the palm of her hand.

Panting with excitement and with the exertion of climbing so many steps, they reached the door of Elspet's flat. The moment she turned the key and opened the door Callum charged straight in and, what was more amazing, he made straight for the kitchen. It *may* have been to make the acquaintance of Eliza ; it *may* have been the appetising smell of dinner. When Elspet followed she found Eliza upon her knees with her arms round the dog and her face transformed beyond all telling.

" Oh, Doctor Mac-Le-od—where *did* you get the doggie ? Isn't he a dear ? Is he ours ? I mean yours, madam ? Oh, won't we just *love* to have him ? "

Callum wagged not only his tail but his entire body. His feelings demanded expression in little " woofs " of delight, and when Eliza, such a happy, excited-looking Eliza, gave him a well-covered bone he fell to with hearty goodwill.

" I'm taking him to some friends in Scotland who have lost their own dog," Elspet explained. " Why, Eliza, I was afraid you would think him a bother."

"A bother, Doctor! Why, I love dogs—especially Scotties, and this flat does need a bit of something to brighten it."

Callum left his bone to make a playful lunge at the heel of her slipper. Then he fell sound asleep in front of the fire. Only every now and then his tail would beat a joyous "tattoo" on the hearthrug.

"Makes you feel as if we 'ad a man in the 'ouse," Eliza said, in a contented voice, bending to rub the muddy footprints off her sacred linoleum.

The doctor had to go out to see some patients afterwards. The weather was still dreary and wet, but her heart was warm within her because she knew that when her work was done she was returning home to where a Scots terrier and a new and astonishingly nice housekeeper were waiting for her.

CHAPTER THIRTEEN

KIRSTY CAMPBELL,
SALESWOMAN

ELIZA and her mistress were having a committee meeting about " What shall we have for dinner ? "

It must be admitted that this consultation was something new—only three weeks old in fact, at which date Callum had taken up his residence with his new friends.

Up till then, Dr. Elspet MacLeod had been more than pleased to leave all arrangements with her efficient housekeeper ; but now Callum had to be catered for and " two heads were better than one," though Elspet had a shrewd suspicion that Eliza had already settled the menu.

" Mutton ? " Elspet suggested.

" We can't have mutton, madam. 'E was ever so sick the last time we 'ad it."

" A nice piece of fresh fish ? "

" Wot about the bones ? Fish and chicken bones should never be given to a dog 'cos they may pierce his eternals."

Eliza had bought a book on the management of dogs and was liable at any odd moment to hurl its contents at her mistress's head.

" Then I think we should have a beefsteak," Elspet said brightly, and as if the idea had only that moment occurred to her. Full well did she know that Eliza had been skilfully leading her up to this very decision.

" I think that'll be best, madam, an' I'll get the butcher to give me a nice marrow bone—bones are good for a dog's teeth." She was evidently still quoting the helpful hints on how to manage a dog.

Suddenly the telephone bell shrilled.

" Hello—yes—the doctor's speaking. *Who?*" Elspet's voice sounded astonished but pleasantly so.

" Yes, of course—only too delighted. Come and have dinner, seven—prompt. By the way, I have a young gentleman friend staying with me just now. I think you'll like him."

There was a pause as if her hearer gasped.

" No, never mind dressing. Of course he always wears tails, but he'll excuse you and me. Good-bye."

Turning to Eliza she said : " That was an old friend from Scotland ringing me up. She's in London just now and I've invited her to dinner. Spread yourself a bit, Eliza ! That orange shape . . .?"

Eliza shook her head sadly but she wasn't really sad ; no, she was glad. Presently she'd put on her coat and hat and, taking Callum with her, she'd do her shopping, and the expedition would be full of thrills for them both. And the tale of Callum's wonderful intelligence and wisdom as related by Eliza would lose nothing in the telling.

The weather had turned dry and frosty ; Christmas was approaching and the shop windows were gay and alluring with " suitable Christmas gifts." Happy secrets looked out of the eyes of the women who were " window shopping " ; presently they would be jaded, and worried, and puzzled, but they hadn't reached that stage yet !

Children in charge of their nurses were trooping past to the park. A rosy baby in a pram smiled at Elspet, and she suddenly felt as if the street were full of bunting and a band were playing somewhere.

She swung along, thinking with pleasure of the day's work in front of her. When " your job is your joy " life is wonderfully worth while. To-day she was due in a school where she had to examine children's eyes.

She and the youngsters were always fast friends ; they told her all sorts of secrets. " Granny gave me these," a small boy confided to her, looking solemnly from behind a pair of steel-rimmed glasses. " These belonged to my grandad, but he's dead now, so granny said I might have them."

Dr. Cumming, with whom she worked at St. Ruth's Hospital, looked at her with twinkling eyes. " You seem very full of beans to-day," he chaffed.

" No wonder, read that." It was a letter from the young wife of the farmer whose eyes had been destroyed by gun-shot.

" We are getting on wonderful," she wrote, " and George is learning to make baskets, my father is teaching him. He's a basket-maker, and I'm to learn, too."

" The pluck of her ! " Elspet said warmly.

We all know days when our work goes " with a bang." To-day was, for Dr. Elspet MacLeod, one of those happy times. On her homeward way she indulged in a packet of Kirsty's favourite cigarettes, some sugar almonds for Callum, and a bunch of tawny chrysanthemums for her own and Eliza's delectation.

She loved to open her outer door now and to wait for the excited scurry of Callum's feet. It was almost worth while to be away from him all day when, at the end of it, he gave one such a joyous welcome—bless his little warm heart ! He had also a most lively interest in any parcel she happened to be carrying and had a perfect passion for sugar almonds. Elspet gave them to him by stealth, as Eliza said, quoting from her book : " Sweets of all kinds are apt to affect a dog's kidneys."

She had just time to arrange her flowers and to cast a look around her pretty sitting-room when Kirsty " breezed " in— no other word can describe her whirlwind entrance.

She was looking her smartest in a swagger coat of bronze brown Harris tweed. A tiny sprig of pressed white heather was stuck in her buttonhole, and in the stitched band of her " hat to match " was a tuft of woodcock's feathers. Beneath her arm she carried a most intriguing-looking flat oblong parcel.

She brought into that tiny London flat a sense of out-of-doorness ; instinctively one

thought of heather hills and singing burns
and the far-off undomestic cry of muir
fowl.

" Elspet, it's good to see you ! "

" Kirsty—come in, my dear." Both girls
spoke at once while Elspet led the way to her
own bedroom.

" Just lay your coat and hat on the
bed."

" Wouldn't you like to know what's in this
parcel ? Don't pretend you haven't noticed
it ! There, you may look ! "

Elspet looked.

" A peat ! " she cried rapturously. " Oh,
Kirsty, you dear ! How did you think of anything so delightful ? I'll set it on fire and put
it in a soup plate on the table."

" You're no better than a pagan woman
burning incense to her gods," Kirsty said with
stern reproof ; all the same she helped her
later on to break the crisp brown peat into
little bits and to set it alight.

" Please praise me for putting on my pretty
new frock," Kirsty cried gaily, " though to
tell the truth I did it to impress your young
gentleman friend. Elspet, I'm shocked ! Has
he been staying for long with you ? What'll
Aunt Eppie say ? "

" Now which question should I answer first? How long has he been here? Three weeks and two days to be exact. What'll Auntie say? I'm sure I don't know. I haven't told her about it yet."

" Produce him instantly," Kirsty commanded.

" All in good time. Eliza's brushing his coat for him and fastening his collar."

Kirsty made a dive for her vanity bag. " I'll need to powder my nose again. Is he—is he—forthcoming? "

" Sometimes," Elspet said gravely. " I've known him to kiss my nose and I've known him to take no notice whatever of me—he's rather aloof sometimes. But Kirsty, you can depend on it, he's always a gentleman."

" Sounds like it," Kirsty agreed dryly.

Then Elspet called : " You may bring him now, Eliza."

The kitchen door was opened and a dignified little Scots terrier with a newly-brushed coat and a tartan collar (which he didn't like) marched solemnly into the room, ears and tail erect.

" Meet Callum ! " Elspet said dramatically.

And Kirsty met him—she went on her knees

to meet him, and she put her arms round his neck.

"You—*moolie!*" she cried, finding her English quite inadequate, and falling back on a Gaelic endearment.

Callum backed away from her. "Forward woman," he said, "I don't know you. Please take no liberties."

But that only made Kirsty more anxious to improve her acquaintance. "Scotties are all like that," she said. "It's what makes them so worth loving."

No one, of course, would ever get Elspet's place in Callum's heart. She had opened the door of his prison house and set him free, but he was willing to take this new friend on trust. He was even willing to "like her fine;" no self-respecting Scottie can go further.

Kirsty, whose brothers kept Scotties, had quite a lot to say about Callum's "points."

"I know," Elspet cried, "he has a pedigree as long as a week, but meantime—*dinner!*"

Kirsty looked around well pleased with her surroundings. "A darling of a room," she said.

Elspet smiled. "Once, not so long ago, it

looked like the waiting-room in a railway station. Soup ? "

The dinner was excellent. Eliza had indeed " spread herself."

" It's pure greed that makes me take a second helping of that orange shape," Kirsty said. " And as you love me and love what's good for me, don't offer me anything more. I tremble for my figure as it is."

" Coffee ? "

" Oh, well, that's different."

The peat had filled the room with the magic and mystery of the moors. The coffee did its share. Content, not to say repletion, was on Callum, who shamelessly went to sleep on Elspet's feet, and in that happy atmosphere the tongues of the exiles wagged sixteen to the dozen.

" Tell me everything about everybody," Elspet said.

" A modest request ! Just to oblige you I'll try to obey you, beginning with myself. I have at the moment a pretty sense of my own importance. May I stick my feet up here ? It makes me feel manly and superior."

" Proceed ! "

" I take it you wish to hear about how and

why I'm in London? D'ye remember Mhairi Matheson from Stornoway? She used to sing at all the Gaelic Mods? No? Well, never mind—she has a little hat shop in Bower Street. Oh, quite a smart little shop! Sports hats and scarves are her specialities. Then, when her customers began to ask where could they get tweed to match their hats, Mhairi wrote to me. I went round a lot of my old cailleachs [1] and got them interested. They'd be delighted to spin and weave and knit. Well, the end of the matter was Mhairi proposed I'd join her—she to take charge of her own department and me—or should I say ' I '?—to take charge of the tweeds." She rose, and with her hand on her heart, made Elspet a profound bow. " You see before you, modom, Christian Campbell, saleswoman at the Highland Tweedshop, Bower Street."

" Congratulations! Splendid! "

" Yes, I think so, too—it's quite a sound scheme. I have three hundred workers' names on my books, all of whom can do something to bring money into homes where they hardly know the colour of it! And we're planning to enlarge the shop. Already we have men's plus-fours, stockings and pull-overs. Every

[1] Old wives.

now and then I swoop down on my workers—
pay for what has been sold—collect a new
supply, and fly back to London with it. I can't
tell you how happy it's making the women,
and, incidentally, I love my job. Elspet, if
you want to see human nature as it really is,
get behind a counter."

"You forget," Elspet reminded her gaily,
"that I have frequently stood behind a
counter in Aunt Eppie's sweetie shop."

"Yes, and sold poisonous treacle beer to
poor unsuspicious young men. By the way,
dear Alice has thrown over Robert Blake.
Yes, she has! She discovered that she only
pitied the poor young man—she didn't really
love him! He had been so passionately in
love with her, she explained, he had quite
swept her off her feet."

"Callum, I really must move my feet—
they're dead," Elspet said, and bent over the
dog to move him a bit. Probably it was the
bending which made her face so flushed when
she raised it. "When did Alice discover
this?" she asked lightly.

"When Uncle Robert Blake, the wealthy
uncle who had one foot in the grave and the
other in a bedroom slipper, suddenly decided
to put both feet into patent pumps in which

to lead his bride—once his nurse—to the altar."

" *Beannich mise !* " Elspet ejaculated. " What happened then ? "

" I'm not quite sure. She's one of our customers, but, of course, I being a mere shopwoman, don't dare to ask questions. She's awfully sweet and patronising to me. I'd like to wring her neck ! " she added vengefully. " By the way, I heard from Lady MacPherson, another of our distinguished customers who isn't at all patronising, that Robert Blake has had to give up work for a while. Whether it's grief over his uncle's marriage or the effect of the blow he got on his head while he was teaching Alice to motor, no one seems to know. Lady MacPherson said he seemed very ill and depressed."

" No wonder," Elspet's voice sounded sympathetic. " Perhaps grief over Alice ? "

" He should thank his stars he has got rid of dear Alice," Kirsty said vehemently. " I'm afraid she's planning to make it up again with Jock MacKintosh—his regiment is ordered home just now. . . . Goodness ! is it so late ? I must fly. Please, Elspet, come and see our shop. You needn't buy anything unless you like ; we'd like to feel you had an interest in us. If you come in on Saturday afternoon, which is our half-day, I'll give you tea and oatcakes and crowdie in the back shop."

" Expect me first Saturday," Elspet cried with a little bubble of excited laughter. " Whatever I may have on—on Saturday—I shall fling away and come."

Kirsty drew herself up haughtily. " We are a respectable firm," she said in stern tones, " and don't ever encourage our customers to fling everything away."

Elspet laughed again ; she was quite unrepentant. Then she said : " I'm glad I haven't your nasty mind."

.   .   .   .

A few days later Elspet got a characteristic letter from Kirsty :

" Just as I thought, my good woman ! My girth is increased by one-sixteenth of an inch, my weight by one and three-quarter ounces ! All your fault for giving me such a dinner. For the rest of this month I shall exist on the smell of an oily rag and the sight of a sour orange !

" As if this was not sufficiently depressing, I had a visit yesterday from Alice Miles, complete with new engagement ring.

" She wished something for a Christmas present, she said, all girlish thrills. Wilfully misunderstanding her, I produced all sorts of feminine wear, including our new crochet lace collars. (Oh, you needn't laugh—they're quite *chic*, let me tell you !)

" ' But—but '—she stammered, ' it's something for my fiancé I want.' ' Ah,' said I, ' let me see now. Mr. Blake is dark—what about a pull-over with orange and tan colouring ? '

" ' The present is not for Mr. Blake,' she said. ' That engagement was a mistake. It was all my fault for mistaking pity for love. What a blessing I found out *before* it was too late ! '

" ' And just *after* his uncle married,' said I sweetly.

" She wanted to slap me, but instead she did quite unnecessary things to her bêret with her bare left hand. Her ring is one of those vulgar, ostentatious affairs ; all huge diamonds and platinum whirlygigs. Her lover has no imagination ! And my dear, it's just as I feared—the victim is poor Jock MacKintosh. She always thought she liked him best ; and after he came into all his grannie's money, she was quite sure.

" So I booked an order for a blue pull-over and a pair of plus-fours stockings to match. You should hear dear Alice haggling about the price ! She could give points to a fishwife any day. I'm nice and catty, aren't I ? I wonder, my dear, if you'd approach your Aunt Eppie to knit the stockings ? I'm *blate* to ask her, but I do want them to be something special, and I know your aunt is a first-class knitter.

" Thanks to dear Alice and her motoring lesson, Robert Blake has disappeared. No one seems to know where he has gone. Let me have a line from you as soon as you hear from Aunt Eppie. Or, better still, come first Saturday and have tea in the back shop.

" Ever thine,

" KIRSTY."

CHAPTER FOURTEEN

THE ELEVENTH HOUR

Work was "throng" in St. Ruth's, and it was only by pulling innumerable strings and by the kindly connivance of Dr. Cumming that Elspet was able to steal away for a couple of days. Had it not been for her promise to Hector MacAulay she would not have attempted it. Eliza, who was broken-hearted at the prospect of losing Callum, went about with a woebegone face.

"If you go on like this, Eliza, I'll have to get another dog for you," Elspet said.

"I don't want another dog," Eliza said reproachfully. "If I can't 'ave Callum I don't want no other."

The train was crowded with holiday makers, cheery but riotous. Christmas gaiety was in the air and Christmas passengers filled to over-flowing the carriages. Callum had to sit on his mistress's knee, much to his annoyance.

When a fellow-traveller sitting opposite began to eat stringy-looking ham sandwiches Callum brightened up and prepared to join the feast. This was entirely his own idea ;

the sandwich-eater munched steadily on and never once said to an anxious-eyed little Scottie : "Would you like a bite?" To the end Callum hoped for the best. Every time the woman opened her mouth to take a bite Callum opened his, too ; but nothing happened. Elspet tried to turn his head towards the window, but he was much too interested in the ham sandwiches to take the least notice of the scenery.

No railway goes near Glen Orrin, and travellers who wish to reach this remote spot have to trust to Colin Cattanach, the mail driver, to give them a lift, and Colin never fails them whatever the capacity of the car may do. On this particular day his car was full to bursting of Christmas parcels. The mail bags bulged mysteriously and the wicker baskets gaped.

"I think if you don't mind sitting on this parcel (it's only Sandy Murray's new suit) you could get room in the front," Colin said, dealing in a masterly way with his load. "That's a living goose going to the school-house, but I don't think she'll bite your legs. Stop you—put your feet up on this stone jar —now, is that any better? You can keep your doggie on your lap."

It was raining ; it had rained steadily all the week, and looked as if it meant to rain for all time and possibly eternity.

" How's everybody ? " Elspet asked.

" We should not complain," Colin said, which is as near as the Highlander will go towards saying everyone's well.

" A few of the old folks are bad with rheumatics," he went on, " and the poor craiturs at Drumcraig are going to the poor-house to-day."

" The poor-house ? " Elspet gasped, her face horrified.

Colin nodded. " It's aaful sad," he said, " but Hector's stone blind now, and his wife hurt her leg on a rusty nail and she didn't look after it, and it's in an aaful mess. They're saying they'll need to take the leg off her, but maybe that's not true. You hear so many queer stories."

Elspet's face was white ; she bit her lips to keep them from trembling. " I suppose this is Doctor Burgess's doings ? " she asked. " What were the neighbours thinking about ? "

" Oh, well, they helped the poor craiturs as well as they could. Old Dolina Gordon was going every day to milk the cow, but they had to sell the cow and I think Lexie gave away all her hens — she hadn't any food for them."

Elspet sighed impatiently. "Put me down at the cross-roads, Colin. Tell my aunt when you're passing that I've gone to see Hector and Lexie, and I'll be home as soon as I can."

" 'Deed—they're telling me your aunt was aaful kind to Lexie and gave her a warm jecket—but Lexie was needing more than a jecket, I'm thinking."

Colin looked admiringly after the young doctor as she swung swiftly along the road to Drumcraig, Callum leaping excitedly at her heels.

" God," she prayed, " don't let me be too late."

The house looked desolate—an ominous silence brooded over the place. The last time Elspet had seen it there were at least the friendly bark of the dog, the cackle of the hens, and the homely " moo " of Rosie, to give some sense of life. But everything was quiet to-day, everything looked ruinous. Even the peat stack, generally the pride of a Highland home, was a tumbled-down heap of sods.

Her heart missed a beat as she stood outside the closed door. The blind was drawn on the ben-end window, and an ancient blue-checked apron of Lexie's shrouded the kitchen one—was she too late?

She listened intently and then she heard Hector speaking. "I've looked in every corner, Lexie, for your new bonnet and I can't find it. There's nothing in this kist but two sheets. Where are you keeping your new boots? There's a long time since I didn't feel them."

Then Lexie's voice, eager and anxious, said: "Stop you, Hector, till I get up. I'll find them—they're maybe in the other kist. Leave the sheets—they're for wrapping round us when we're dead——"

She burst into bitter tears. "Oh, Hector, to think that we would live to see the day that we have to be going to *yon place*! And us that could always hold up our heads with the best of them!"

"We'll not go," Hector said, sudden grim resolve in his voice.

"But we must go," Lexie said. "It's for our good; the doctor says so. You'll be getting baker's bread every day. See to that now! And maybe they can do something for my sore leg."

"I would like better a dry farle and a drink

of cold water in our own house," he said drearily.

"Hush," Lexie warned. "I'm thinking I'm hearing the doctor. He said he would look in if he had time, and he would send the ambulance." She raised her voice and called : "Be coming in, Doctor. We're—we're—very —near—ready."

The fire had been allowed to go out—a terribly significant thing in the Highlands where a fire may "rest" but must not die. The dark little room was full of the smell of dead things : dead fires—dead hopes—dead hearts.

The newcomer stood for a moment till her eyes got used to the gloom and she could distinguish Lexie sitting in the box-bed.

"My dears ! " Elspet said, and burst into tears, her arms wrapped close round the little old bewildered woman.

"Who — who —— " Lexie stammered. "Lassie, is it yourself? Surely the Lord sent you just in time. . . . Oh, Elspet—they're taking us to *yon place* the day ! "

"No, they're not then ! " Elspet flung back gaily, though it cost her a huge effort to be gay. "Certainly not ! I say so."

"Wait a moment—we must have **more**

light." With one quick jerk she had the window uncovered. " Your fire has gone out," she cried. " Dear, dear ! I must light it at once. And how are you both keeping ? Have you forgotten that I'm hoping to help Hector to see again ? "

" No," said Hector, " but we thought *you* had."

" That's all the faith you have in me." She was still gay, but she found it necessary to run outside for just a moment. She said it was to look for a piece of kindling wood. Perhaps.

There was an old whin bush at the foot of the garden ; she began feverishly to break off its branches, trying all the time to wink back her tears.

" Let me do that for you," said a voice at her back, and Robert Blake put out his strong, brown, capable-looking hands to help.

" Oh, Robert ! " she said, forgetful of the fact that she had never so addressed him before. " Doctor Burgess is wanting to send Hector and Lexie to the poor-house—and he mustn't be allowed."

" Of course he mustn't," he said firmly, his voice warm and friendly. Then their eyes met and there was in them the perfect intimacy of a perfect understanding.

" A great girl like you shouldn't be crying," he went on, a teasing note in his voice, and a tender light in his eye, " especially when you don't seem to have a hanky. Here, take mine and I'll carry in the sticks. By the way, what are they for ? "

She explained. It took a little time, though " we measure time by heart-beats not by figures on a dial." When they re-entered the little home, Dr. Burgess was standing in the middle of the kitchen floor and Lexie, in the miraculous way in which women do these things, had suddenly grown quite aloof and dignified and was giving the doctor his marching orders.

" No, thank you, Doctor Burgess," she was saying in her best English, " our own doctor, Doctor MacLeod, is going to look after us and we're staying where we are."

Elspet did not see Dr. Burgess's outstretched hand. He did not care to meet the righteous anger blazing in her eyes.

" Was this necessary, Doctor Burgess ? Haven't they both the old-age pension ? "

" It wasn't enough, I did it for the best," he muttered. " They needed someone to look after them and they'd be much better in the poor-house. I think you're making a mistake."

Lexie shuddered. The very name "poor-house" made her grue and she would never pronounce it; she referred to it as "*yon place.*"

The doctor took his departure, and Callum, who had been an interested onlooker all this time, thought that now someone should take notice of him. Elspet lifted him up and put him on Lexie's lap whilst she and Robert Blake battled with wet sticks, wetter peats, and a box of matches. They succeeded at last in getting the fire started.

"Your good luck is back to-day, Lexie," Elspet cried. "Look how cheery the fire is!"

Poor blind Hector sitting in his chair crept nearer the fire and spread out his hands to the welcome blaze.

"Where is your well, Lexie?" Elspet asked, seizing a water pail.

"Hector can take in the water," Lexie cried. "Many's the pail he has carried in for me since I have been laid up."

It was quite true; that strange sixth sense which comes to the blind had come to Hector and he could grope his way with wonderful accuracy. He was as pleased as a child when he could do any little thing to help, and Lexie praised him as if he were indeed a child.

Over the empty cupboard the eyes of the young folk met in consternation. There was no food in the house. "I have 'Biddy'—she's all new and mended—and if you tell me what to get I'll go to the shop and get it," Robert Blake whispered. There was a delightful sense of intimacy in the consultation. He handed her a page out of his note-book and a lead pencil and watched with great interest the first specimen he had ever seen of Elspet's characteristic handwriting.

Nothing to be sentimental about, one would think? Only those who have never known the glamour which love casts would so speak. The words upon which his eyes rested so tenderly were : " A quarter-pound of tea ; a pound of sugar ; a loaf ; half a pound of butter ; a tin of condensed milk ; and an ounce of bogie roll tobacco ! " Prosaic enough, yet because of the story behind them they were magical and wonderful.

He read the words as if they were a love-letter—he pressed his lips to them when he thought no one was looking, and then he tenderly put the leaf into his breast pocket.

CHAPTER FIFTEEN

THE GAELIC STUDENT

ELSPET will always look back with a thrill on that Christmas holiday, though anything less like a holiday or less like Christmas one could not imagine. But it was "one crowded hour of glorious life"!

Aunt Eppie had resurrected the red rowans from their grave in the garden and had mixed them with sprigs of holly. Despite the un-Christmas-like weather there was the unmistakable Christmas spirit abroad, and it was not till Elspet, with her aunt and Robert Blake, were sitting down to dinner that it occurred to her to ask him : "What are *you* doing here? And how did you know I was in Drumcraig?"

"Colin, the carrier, told your aunt, who told me, so 'Biddy' and myself thought we'd run along and see if we could help you. And I *did* help you," he said. "You'd never have lighted that fire if I hadn't helped you."

"Don't boast," she said coldly. "Perhaps you think I did not notice that you tore up

the whole of a book to get that fire to go. **And**
it was my *Romance of War*, too."

"I'll buy you another," he promised.
"May I have another potato?"

She eyed him sternly. "Someone told me
you were ill and depressed," she said.

He laid down his knife and fork in order to
laugh properly.

"*Ill, depressed!*" he spluttered. "What do
you say about this, Miss MacLeod?" He
turned to Aunt Eppie, with whom he seemed
to be on most familiar terms.

She helped him to another slice of chicken
and a spoonful of stuffing. Robert Blake
swallowed what was in his mouth—took a
deep breath and then uttered a series of most
alarming sounds.

"Do you understand that?" he asked.

Elspet looked at him, in alarm. "I thought
you were choking," she said.

"I was speaking Gaelic," he explained in a
hurt voice. "Your aunt is teaching me and I
said just now 'A merry Yuletide and a happy
Hogmanay.'"

"I'm glad to know it," Elspet said fervently.
"I was afraid you——"

"That I was going potty?" he asked
cheerfully. "Not a bit. I'm glad the doctor

who ordered me to take a long rest can't see
me. He'd be chasing me back to my job. As
it is, I'm living in the Lodge, with old Granny
Fergusson to ' do ' for me and finding the
days all too short for the number of things
I have to do. I'm learning Gaelic (you heard
me), I can play the harp—the Jews' harp—
a little," he said modestly, " and I intend
taking up the melodion. If I knew where
' Melodion Nannie ' is I might get her to help."

Elspet smiled, but next moment she sighed.
" In the meantime we must see what's to be
done about Lexie and Hector. I must go
and have a talk with them presently. Perhaps
I was rash when I said I'd look after them.
I wonder if you could take Hector for a little
walk, Mr. Blake, so that I could have a quiet
talk with Lexie and find out about things."

" I'll go, but on one condition," he said
firmly.

" What's that—you haggler ? "

" That you call me ' Robert ' again." And
she agreed.

Lexie had given Elspet a glimpse of her
inner life on a former occasion, but the story
she told Elspet that evening was infinitely
sadder.

She had practised on poor Hector, during

his years of oncoming blindness, all sorts of little deceits.

" I was sometimes glad he was not seeing how things were going against me," Lexie whispered. "Are you sure, *m'eudail*, the door is shut? Well-a-well, after you went back to London, Rosie fell ill and she dropped her calf. We had to get the vet. from Weir Bridge—that's twenty miles away—and it cost money—much money—and then there were medicines and things for poor Rosie. . . . When she got better, I had not the food for her . . . and I had to sell her. . . ." She was silent, her work-worn old hands picking aimlessly on the bed-cover.

" I told Hector I had put her away just for the winter and that she would be coming back in the spring when we had the new grass.

" Everything went against me after that. Myself was thinking the Almighty was punishing me for telling lies, but I only did it to spare Hector. Then the butcher's van killed Glen, my poor dog. I was glad in a way, for I had no food for him, and then I hurt my leg—just a scratch from a rusty nail in the pitchfork . . . and now look at it."

Elspet examined the wound; she had been prepared for something very bad. Colin

Cattanach had said : " They're saying the leg must come off her." But it wasn't so bad as that, though it was bad enough !

" I'll just clean it and dress it, Lexie, you go on and tell me the rest ; and don't, for pity's sake, think God was punishing you."

" My blessings on you, my dearie," the old woman said. " No, no, I'm not heeding the pain—I'm not heeding anything now that you have come and the Lord has sent you. But would you say, like a good lass, to Hector, that his eyes are not ready to be cut ? " She looked anxiously into Elspet's face. " Say you to him that it will be better to wait till the spring, and by that time "—she lowered her voice—" if the Lord spares me I'll be able to get about again and I'll see if I couldn't get one or two of the lads to help me to put down the crop . . . and maybe . . . I could get a young *quay* (cow), and I'll set a clocking hen and get chickens, and Dolina Gordon will give me a puppy."

Elspet listened with a worried look. " Do you think Hector'll be very disappointed ? " she asked.

" Not so disappointed as if he got his eyes only to see everything going to rack and ruin. And hasn't myself been telling the poor man a pack of lies—saying I had a new bonnet and new boots, and all that's in that kist are the dead clothes—the shrouds and the jacket your auntie sent me ? " She covered her face with her shaky hands, a tragic, pitiful, little old woman.

Elspet felt herself on the " horns of a dilemma." When Hector and Robert Blake returned, she ordered Robert to rebuild the peat stack whilst she dealt with Hector's eyes.

" Bring in an armful of peats and let them dry in front of the fire," she commanded, and Robert uttered more strange words. " That's Gaelic," he announced.

" What is it in English ? "

" It's a fine day, Your Majesty."

" I'm glad to hear it. Now, Hector, you and I will go to the ben-end and I'll have a look at your eyes. Just sit here near the window. Now let me look——" there was a queer, tense feeling in the room. Elspet adjusted the instruments she had brought ; her face was anxious.

" You're ever so much better than the last time I saw you," she said in the cheerful tones of the professional. " And your eyes are getting on well, but . . . we'll just wait till spring before removing the cataract . . . I *could*, of course, do it now, but it'll make a better job if we wait till February or March, so that when you see the world again it'll be wearing its new spring dress of green."

There was something infinitely pathetic in the way he submitted. " Very well, my lass," he said patiently. He was not by nature a patient man—far from it. This made his submission all the more pathetic. " If you're saying that, then I'll wait."

" It won't be long," Elspet said, determined to be cheerful.

" Oh, no," he agreed listlessly. Then he burst out—the old fierce spirit would no longer be restrained.

" It's Lexie," he said. " She's telling me she has this and that in the house, and that the cow is away for the winter only, and I'm wondering—I'm wondering *is it true?* "

" You've got the best wife in the world and the bravest, and *that's* true," Elspet reassured him. " Come along now back to the kitchen and we'll tell her all about it."

" And we're not going to *yon place?* " Hector said as one who counts his blessings.

" No," Elspet rejoined, " and you're going to help me to nurse Lexie."

" Lexie," she said, guiding Hector to his chair, " we could remove the cataract just now, but Hector and I have decided to wait till the spring, and so make a better job of it."

Lexie was sure this was the wisest thing. " Once my leg is healed up——" she began.

" And Rosie back," Elspet put in, with a warning look at the old woman.

" Oh, yes," Lexie said, rather breathlessly.

" I'm going to see the district nurse and get her to come and dress your leg after I go away. I don't see why Doctor Burgess didn't send her here long ago."

" He was thinking we would be less bother if he sent us to *yon place*," Lexie whispered.

" There are one or two other things I must see to in the clachan." She looked inquiringly at Robert Blake.

" ' Biddy ' and I wait your pleasure," he said gallantly.

Elspet will never be a rich woman ; her money always burns a hole in her pocket, but she will always be rich in friends. She never has the smallest scruple about roping them in to help her in her schemes. The old minister in Greenhill, a saint, but one who lived so far away that he did not know what was happening in the outposts of his parish, she went to see first. It was always a sore spot with him that Dr. Burgess did not tell him of cases where he might help.

"But I'll look after them now, Doctor MacLeod," he assured Elspet.

So before she slept that night she had got matters at Drumcraig on a new footing.

"The Lord sent you," Lexie whispered. "It was the eleventh hour that He sent you—He wasn't late."

.   .   .   .

When Elspet returned to London, Callum occupied her lap again. Robert Blake motored her to the railway station, and although he said no word of love, "the love licht was in his e'e."

"May I write?" he asked.

"Please do—keep me posted up about Hector and Lexie."

"Is that all you wish to hear?"

"Oh, well, you may let me know how you're getting on with your Gaelic."

"I shall," he said fervently. "I'm told there's no language like it for love-making."

The whistle shrieked.

" Give my love to London and tell it I'll be back in April or May." Then he uttered some strange words. When thinking over them as the train sped on its way, it dawned on Elspet that what he was trying to say was : " *Failte dhut 'us Slainte leat,*" which being translated means " Hail to thee and farewell."

CHAPTER SIXTEEN

HEATHER ALE

THE festive season, with its over-eating and over-drinking, was passed, and the depression which wrapped everyone around was due quite as much to indigestion as to the weather. The doctors were kept busy and Dr. Elspet MacLeod had scarcely a moment to herself. She, for some strange reason, was not suffering from depression. She said it was because Callum had such a delightful influence in the house, turning it from a mere house with a robot caretaker into a home with a sympathetic and wholly human housekeeper.

She hurried in one evening to find Kirsty Campbell settled by her fire with Callum in close attendance.

" Kirsty ! How delightful to see you ! "

" While you're hugging me you can run your hands over my pockets and see if there's a bulge in any of them. If there's not, and you're still glad to see me, I'll begin to think there's something in friendship."

" I've hugged you—I've felt for a bulge,

146

and there isn't one, and I'm *still* glad to see you," Elspet said, reproachfully.

" 'Tis well—you may let your eye dwell on that parcel on your table—a bap and a finnan haddie sent to me this very day from Scotland."

Elspet rang the bell. " Supper is indicated," she said. " Look, Eliza, what Miss Campbell has brought us ! On with your frying-pan instantly ! Don't spare the butter on the bap when you've toasted it, and, above all, hurry ! "

Having issued these exciting orders, Elspet and her visitor settled themselves comfortably in chairs by the fire.

With her feet on the side of the mantel-piece, Kirsty said : " Do you realise that I haven't seen you since you ran off to Scotland ? By the way, Elspet, I must congratulate you on your good looks. What have you been doing to yourself ? Oh, no, you'll never be a beauty, but you have your moments of looking —how shall I put it ? "

" No' so bad," Elspet suggested.

" Something like that ; it's as if a lamp were lighted inside you and the light is shining out of your eyes."

" Like a turnip lantern ? " Elspet hinted.

Kirsty gave her a haughty look. " The conversaton now ceases," she declared, and shut her eyes. She opened them next minute however, to say : " And I was trying so hard to be nice to you."

" And I appreciate your attempts. If I weren't so hungry I'd appreciate them even more. I wish Eliza would be quick with the supper, for I haven't tasted a genuine ' finnan ' for donkey's years."

" Don't forget the bap, too."

" I don't ; I'm saying grace for it. And, by the same token, here's Eliza." She sniffed appreciatively. " The very smell is doing me good," she announced.

It was a merry, informal, and thoroughly indigestible meal, served on a little gate-legged table drawn up near the fire, with the teapot sitting sociably on a stand inside the copper curb.

" By rights," said Kirsty, " we should have heather ale instead of tea."

" It wouldn't be nearly so nice as tea," Elspet said, refilling her cup.

" But what I came to say, however," Kirsty went on, " is a big thank-you to your Aunt Eppie for knitting the stockings. I feel I must almost call them ' *hose*.' They were so beautiful and Alice liked them so much I was almost afraid she was going to keep them for herself. ' Only I've got such a long, slender foot,' she explained. By the way, is it true your aunt has got a Gaelic pupil? Alice hinted as much, but I don't know where she got her information. To believe her, Robert Blake is still so hopelessly in love with her he can't bear to leave the place where he met her."

Elspet's eyes flashed angrily. " She's a liar," she said grimly, " and you may tell her so from me. Robert Blake, thanks to her recklessness in wrecking his car, has injured his head——"

" It was always cracked," Kirsty interposed, softly.

Without pretending to hear her, Elspet went on : ". . . so badly that every now and then he's prostrated with headaches. He didn't tell me this. To believe him he's riotously well, but Aunt Eppie told me the truth. The only thing that helps him is absolute quiet and that's why he's in the Glen. For nights and nights he can't get a wink of sleep, and he goes for long tramps among the hills when other folk are in their beds. I could *shake* that wretch ! She has managed to wreck his life pretty effectively, and to speak like that makes me physically sick."

Kirsty looked at her with a speculative eye. " So that's how you feel about Robert Blake, is it ? "

" Yes, that's how I feel." Elspet's voice was trembling. " I care for him and I believe he cares for me, but Heaven only knows if he'll ever tell me so ! "

A silence fell on the friends, but it was an understanding silence.

Then the conversation swung round to the other dwellers in the Glen, and Elspet told with great humour that Aunt Eppie and Robert Blake were trying to brew heather ale. She told her, too, about Hector and Lexie and how very nearly they had gone to the poor-house.

" Sandy Morrison is sending Rosie back to them whenever Lexie's well enough to milk her. No, I didn't leave Callum with her, after all. Lexie's getting a collie pup from a neighbour, and that will be more use. Callum, of course, sighs for the wide, open spaces with rabbits to chase and cats to send flying up trees. But there are compensations—there is Eliza ! Her joy over his return was rather touching. Poor Eliza ! "

Next morning's post brought a letter with

the Glen Orrin postmark. It was the first time Elspet had seen Robert Blake's writing, and it thrilled her. It was so exactly like him she'd have known it anywhere. For quite five seconds she studied the firm handwriting with its straight up and down lines, and then she slit the envelope and read her first love-letter.

It did not seem like a love-letter, though anyone like Elspet who could read between the lines could easily recognise it as such.

Robert wrote :

" DEAR DOCTOR,

" According to promise, I now send you a report on your three invalids : Hector, Lexie, and Robert (oh, yes, he's really your patient and the one who needs you most).

" Well, as I was saying, we're getting along nicely. Hector's developing a perfectly wonderful sense of locality and he often takes me long treks. One day we actually reached that hikers' bothy along the main road and got there by all manner of by-paths.

" Lexie's leg (I hope I am not indelicate in mentioning it) is healing up splendidly, and as for me, I can now play on the harp (Jew's) the three opening bars of ' My Love She's but a Lassie Yet.' MacDougall does not think much of my playing. I seem to remember he did not think much of yours either. And now, the honours being equal, I hope that by the time you return I'll be able to play the whole tune with suitable expressions, both facial and musical. I am also helping your aunt to make *heather ale*. The genuine, authentic stuff—none of your treacle beer !

"When all other means of earning a livelihood fail me I hope to turn an honest penny by selling heather ale and playing on the harp. How do you like the idea of my becoming a wandering minstrel ? 'Melodion Nannie' is one, you know.

"Your aunt is very well. She says I'm getting on with my Gaelic. I hope she says this because it's true and not because she thinks I'd like her to say it. Read that sentence three times over so as to grasp its meaning, and meantime believe me, dear Doctor MacLeod,

"Your obedient patient,

"ROBERT BLAKE."

CHAPTER SEVENTEEN

THE HIKERS' BOTHY

THE snow which should have come at Christmas came instead in February. Snow in London is always a mistake ; it may intend to turn the city into a fairy town, but it only succeeds in making wet pavements and slushy streets.

Influenza came in its train, too, influenza which with the slightest encouragement turned into pneumonia. In one of the private wards in St. Ruth's, where Miss Fraser, the wealthy Scottish lady, had been battling for her life, the tide turned, and after a stiff fight she was pronounced out of danger.

She begged that Dr. MacLeod, who had stood by her in her illness, would see her safely home to Inverness. Dr. Cumming, looking at the weary face of his colleague, seconded the motion.

" Go and take a week's holiday," he suggested. " You'll work all the better for a breather just now. You know I don't want to be bothered with a sick partner, and I think I know where I could get a locum.

Just oblige me by going. I'm making all
arrangements about travelling, and believe me,
young woman, you'll travel like Royalty."

Elspet smiled. She was desperately tired,
and for some obscure reason there was a great
urge upon her spirit to visit Glen Orrin. If
she went to Inverness it would be an easy
matter to dash for a few days to the Glen
and assure herself that all there were well.
Aunt Eppie had been father and mother to her
ever since her own parents had died of this
same terrible type of influenza as was now
sweeping over the land. What if her aunt
should take it? And there were others in the
Glen. . . .

By the end of the month the invalid was able
to be moved, and Elspet did indeed travel
like a royal personage to Inverness. Let no
one despise money ; in times of illness it can
work magic, and can help a patient to make a
good recovery. Elspet was able to hand over
her patient to the Inverness doctor and nurse,
none the worse for her long journey.

She had rather a rush to catch her own
train ; in fact, had it been up to time she
wouldn't have managed it.

The guard took possession of her suitcase.
" It's all right, mem," he said, " here you are,

a corner seat. Muirtown? I'm glad you're not going farther, for the line is blocked at Bonar Bridge."

After the warmth and luxury of the " special," Elspet felt cold and shivery. She wished she had told her aunt she was coming. Had she done so, it was wildly possible that Robert Blake and " Biddy " might have come to meet her. She was almost as anxious about Blake as she was about her aunt, for Aunt Eppie had said he seemed to be spending his time taking long tramps among the hills, often with Hector MacAulay as companion. She knew from that that he was having trouble with his head and that he was sleepless.

Colin Cattanach, burly in a huge grey coat and with the flaps of his cap tied under his chin, was waiting on the platform for the mails. He shook his head when he saw the young doctor. " The train is late," he said, " and I'm thinking, Doctor, you should stay here. My mail-car is broken down—I have only a horse and gig the day."

She laughed the idea to scorn. " There's not much snow here," she said. Colin looked at the grey, lowering sky. " It's like a heavy fall," he said, anxiously. " And when I came east this morning the roads were none too good, especially between Glen Orrin and the Kelpie's Brig."

He piled the back of the gig with luggage and mail-bags so as to give them a little shelter. The station-master's wife gave them a cup of hot tea and Elspet climbed up beside Colin, impatient to be off.

There were eighteen miles between her and Aunt Eppie. She looked anxiously at her watch. Twelve o'clock! When would they reach their journey's end? The odd thing was that never for a single instant did she repent this rash and cold journey! When Colin again suggested that she should stay in Muirtown she looked quite angry.

"Have it your own way," Colin said in a resigned voice. He had not been a mail-driver for the last score of years without knowing the difficulty of making a *thrawn* woman body change her mind!

He tucked Elspet in as snugly as he could, lighted his pipe, gathered up the reins, spoke an encouraging word to the horse, and they were off!

"They're all fine in the Glen, so far as I know," he said in reply to Elspet's question, "How is everybody?" "There's a couple living in the hikers' bothy and they're telling me the young wife is not very well. Indeed, I have a bottle of medicine for her in my pocket."

The road for the first ten miles was sheltered ; after that it ran parallel to the river and began to climb higher and higher. They could hear the angry stream dashing seaward between steep rocky banks.

The air was now full of whirling snowflakes ; had Colin not known the way, they might have fared dangerously. Every here and there he had to stop at some farmhouse or some wayside cottage to deliver a letter or a newspaper, or a parcel. Progress was slow. Elspet glanced at her watch. She was chilled to the bone. To make matters worse, a gale of wind was sweeping from the bens, blinding horse and driver with snow. But still they held doggedly on their way. Time was getting on, it was nearly three o'clock.

Suddenly, an ominous grinding sound, accompanied by a violent shaking of the gig, alarmed them.

" *Beannich mise !* " Colin muttered. He handed the reins to Elspet while he climbed down to examine things. His hands were so numbed it took him quite a while to discover what was wrong.

" I'm aaful sorry, Doctor," he said, " but it's the axle of the hind wheel. We're not far from the hikers' bothy and I think we should try to reach it."

" I'd better get out," she said. On the whole, she was glad to get her frozen feet below her again. " And what now ? " she asked, stamping her feet to promote circulation.

" I'll put the mails on Diamond's back and leave the gig at the roadside. If you'll walk behind me, I'll try to shelter you, and I'll carry your suitcase."

More time was spent over this arrangement, and the short winter day was beginning to close, while the cold was intense. Diamond, poor, patient beast, led the way. Colin, with his hand on His Majesty's mails to keep them from falling off the horse's back, came next, and Elspet followed with her leather coat tucked up, putting careful feet into Colin's footprints.

" There's the light of the bothy," Colin said. " Cathal Stewart is the man's name, He's a woodcutter from Badenoch." In the whirling snow Elspet had some difficulty in catching a glimpse of the light. On such a night, to see a friendly light and to know that human beings are behind it is wonderfully comforting. Both

" You get me lots of boiling water. I'll need gallons, and do you think you could get your wife and me a cup of tea ? "

" I'll—do—whatever—you—ask—me," he gasped. " Is she——"

" She'll be all right soon," she assured him. " Keep the house as quiet as you can."

He stole on tiptoe from water-butt to hearth and back again for an armful of sticks, ever keeping an anxious ear pricked for sounds from the " other end," where the Angels of Life and Death were brushing wings.

There was a cheap little clock on the mantel-piece. Again and again he glanced at it. Did ever time crawl by so slowly ?

The wind had died down, and when he looked out it seemed as if all the world were sleeping beneath a thick blanket of snow. He stood miserably looking up and down the quiet, lovely world. There was no moon, but the stars were shining and the sight of them calmed his spirit.

Then he began to listen. Sounds would carry far to-night. Wasn't that the sound of men's voices ?

Yes . . . and there were men, a crowd of them, coming straight towards the bothy. They came from the Glen Orrin direction.

He went a few steps towards them, mindful of the doctor's injunctions about quietness. Rory, the stalker from the head of the Glen, was the first he met. "Did you see a young man passing along this way?" he asked.

"A doctor? A man doctor?"

"No, no—the gent that's living in the Lodge. He's been out since last night and they're afraid he's lost. He went for a walk in the hills, and with the snow coming on we're afraid he's lost his way."

Cathal shook his head. He had seen no such man. Had he not been so worried about his young wife he'd have offered to join the search-party.

Rory shook him warmly by the hand. "Man, man! when it comes to your sixth or seventh you'll think nothing of it," he assured him, speaking as one who knows; and then the searchers went on their way.

Back in the bothy, Cathal stole another glance at the clock. Surely time was standing still. He could hear guarded movements in the " other end," and once the door opened and an anxious voice asked :

"What man is lost in the snow? I heard the men speaking."

" The gent that's living in the Lodge," he replied. " I do not know his name."

Did he imagine it, or was there a sound like a strangled gasp? Silence fell on the troubled little house. Cathal boiled kettle after kettle and listened outside the shut door, and then he went out into the starry night. Waiting is the hardest work in the world.

How still the world was—full to the brim of silence. That little tapping noise he heard—what was it? He peered along the road and saw by the stars' shine, the figure of an old man tapping the ground cautiously, but stepping along as if the way were quite familiar. He made straight for the bothy door, and then he sensed Cathal's presence.

" I beg your pardon," he said, courteously. " I did not know anyone was staying in the bothy."

" We have been staying here for a month," Cathal replied. " I'm one of the woodcutters. The others are staying in the big bothy at the Kelpie's Brig, but because I am married they gave me this hikers' bothy, and to-night the wife—I cannot be asking you in—you'll excuse me, if you please."

" I could not wait, in any case," Hector MacAulay said, simply. " I'm looking for the young man from the Lodge—he's lost and I have a notion that I can find him. I took him here one day. You see, day and night are all the same to me. I'm praying the Almighty that I may not be too late." He turned and then spoke again with simple dignity. " I'm wishing you and your young wife all blessings. Have you help for the poor creature ? "

" Aye, the doctor's here with her, a lady doctor."

The blind man stood as one arrested. " A lady doctor ? " he echoed. " Is she of the name of MacLeod ? " His voice was warm.

" Yes, I am." It was Elspet herself who spoke. " Hector, I cannot wait to speak to you, for there is much for me to do here. I cannot leave this woman in her hour, so I'm trusting you, Hector, to find Robert Blake and bring him back to me."

" I will that, my lass," he replied. He murmured to himself, " And may the Supreme Being grant that I'll find him living."

Midnight was striking when Elspet carried a little, red-faced morsel of humanity and laid him in his daddy's arms. " It's a boy," she said, triumphantly, and returned to minister to the weary young mother. She had her sleeves rolled up and her arms wet and soapy when her arch enemy, Dr. Burgess, arrived, and with him the district nurse. It says much for her state of nerves that she was actually glad to see him.

"The man is in the National Health Insurance, so we'll get the maternity grant all right," he told her. Elspet was too tired to answer him as she would have liked to do. Now that her anxiety about the young mother and her baby was over, she had time to think of her own private anxieties. Had she found Robert Blake only to lose him again? But Hector—she had a queer feeling that Hector would find him. She wished she had not overheard Hector's parting words: "May the Supreme Being grant that I'll find him living."

"God grant it," she breathed, and turned to answer Dr. Burgess's questions and to hand the baby over to the nurse.

In this quiet hour of midnight, when even Nature seemed to be holding her breath, there was a step at the door, a hand fumbled for the sneck, and old Hector stumbled in.

"I have found him," he said. "He's yonder at the burn side. No, he's not——" He jibbed at a word no Highlander will willingly utter. "He's still spared—he was

165

breathing—but we must go quickly for him."

Elspet was already buttoning her coat. "You'll come with us, Doctor Burgess," she said. "Is it far off, Hector?"

"No, about half a mile. It's on the short cut from the Glen to this bothy—wasn't it myself that showed him the way? He liked to be coming because he said the view was so grand."

Into some days are crowded the doings of a year—thus it was with this queer day. The searchers now reappeared very down-heartedly. They could get no trace of the missing man. They were met by the joyous news that a blind old man had succeeded where they had failed.

The hikers' bothy was full of joy, and Cathal could not resist telling his news.

"There's a little one come since you saw us last," he said.

"Well done—a lassie?" asked Rory.

"No, then; guess again."

"A boy?"

"Quite right," Cathal said, much too excited to be conscious of the fact that Rory was shamelessly "pulling his leg."

"You'll give us all a thimbleful of the 'craitur' when we come back?"

" I will that," said Cathal, and the searchers, led by Hector, fared forth once more. Dr. Burgess went with them, and he insisted that Elspet should stay and rest ; amazing consideration !

It was her turn now to watch the deliberate passing of time. The young mother and child were both sleeping, the nurse was doing things in the " other end," the fire blazed cheerily, and she was conscious of an overwhelming tiredness. She leant her head against the side of the fireplace and fell sound asleep.

It was Hector who wakened her with a gentle hand on her shoulder. " *M'eudail*," he said, " we have found him, and we're taking him home in the doctor's car, and we think you should be coming, too."

She stumbled to her feet, blinking sleepily. For a moment she was too bewildered to remember things. Then memory woke.

" Is Mr. Blake all right, Hector ? "

" He is that. He's got another crack on his head, but he was able to scold me for coming to look for him. He's hurt his leg, but he'll soon be all right."

Outside in the quiet white night they were waiting for her. They made room for her in

the back seat where Robert Blake had already
been placed.

" How badly do you think he's hurt ? " she
asked Dr. Burgess.

" Just a knock on the head—possibly some
bruises and a sprained ankle. You sit beside
him."

Blake seemed hardly conscious and suddenly
swayed towards her shoulder. She put her
arm round him and tenderly whispered :
" *M'eudail !* "

With her arm still around the half-conscious
man she looked back at the hikers' bothy. It
was a place and a night which would live for
ever in her memory.

CHAPTER EIGHTEEN

FEBRUARY-FILL-THE-DYKES

THE old folk-word that February fills the dykes and March empties them did not come true that year, for by the last day of the month the snow had vanished, leaving the world looking green and fresh. " I'm glad to see you," said the blue sky, looking down at the loch. The loch returned the compliment with a flash of blue water. Everywhere there was the sound of singing rivers and burns. Such magic words as " fishing-rods," " reels," " trout " and " salmon " were borne on the air where men met each other.

" Let's get up and go somewhere," murmured the breeze.

Elspet heard the message and sighed. " I must go back to my work," she thought. Spring in London is not the glamorous thing it is in the Highlands of Scotland. She bent to examine the first brave snowdrop which was pushing its head through the earth, and as she did so the tiny sprig of rowans she had taken from the bunch on the dresser fell out of her waist-belt. It seemed a curious meeting of the seasons, and again she sighed.

A little red motor-car came flying along the road, sending up cascades of muddy water in its wake.

Elspet eyed it and its driver severely. " *Amadan*," she murmured.

Her displeasure had not the slightest effect on the motorist who was coming jauntily (albeit rather limpingly) along the garden path.

" Can you tell me how far it is to the hikers' bothy ? " he asked, raising his cap and ignoring her frown.

" You are eight miles from it," she replied with cold politeness, " and five from the Lodge where you should still be in bed. I thought you had a cracked head and a twisted ankle ? "

" Entirely your own idea," he replied airily. " I suppose there is no place hereabouts where a man could get a drink of—of—beer ? "

" My aunt sells beer : treacle, ginger, and herb," she answered, demurely. " If you will come into the shop, I'll get you a glass. Treacle beer, I think I remember, was your former choice ? "

Then their eyes met and they burst into laughter, and after that there was no use for

Elspet to try to be stand-offish. But she still felt she should reproach him.

"You have no business to be careering about the country already."

He looked subdued—at least he tried to look subdued, though anyone could see he was bursting to impart some happy secret.

"Do you know, Doctor, something wonderful has happened to my head. The crack seems to have joined up, and the horrid weight which was always over my eyes has gone. So have the sleeplessness and the misery. You that are a medical genius—can you explain the mystery?"

She gave him a shrewd look—he certainly looked a different being from the last time she had seen him. "What do you think yourself?" she asked in true Scots fashion.

"I think that the thing I call my brain had gone into low gear with the first knock and the second knock pushed it back into normal—how about it? Told by the village idiot in words of one syllable," he went on, joyously. "Anyway, I'm feeling fine and so is 'Biddy,' and we want you to stick on your hat and coat and come for a run. It's your duty to pay a visit to the youngest inhabitant of the Glen."

Aunt Eppie, who had joined them, warmly agreed.

The world seemed an exceedingly wonderful place that morning.

" Isn't it strange how the weather has the power to make us miserable or happy ? " Elspet asked as they sped along.

" And are you happy ? " Robert asked.

" Yes, the day is so lovely," she explained, lest he might misunderstand the reason of her happy face.

Gaiety was in the air ; there was no use trying to be serious, though Elspet did make one or two worthy attempts. But what is one to do when one's companion refuses to be serious also ?

" I'm glad my last day is so good," she went on. " To-morrow I return to my sadly-neglected duties."

" And I also," he replied. " I'm going to see my doctor and shall bully him into saying I'm all right again. After we see the youngest inhabitant, would you like to see the spot where Hector found me ? As yet no cross marks it, but just wait. . . ."

" Hector is already frightfully angry at the amount of publicity you have brought him ! Just to keep his mind occupied, I have been telling him of our plans for his operation at Easter. It's to be done in Inverness. Robert," she said softly, " I want to thank you for your kindness to my old couple."

He made alarming sounds in his throat, and when she gave him a startled look he explained that he was telling her in Gaelic that if she referred to the subject again he would throw her out of the car.

" I think after this that we'd better stick to English. It will save misunderstandings," she said, meekly.

" Just as you like," he agreed and sounded his horn, which brought out the father of the youngest inhabitant with a scared face.

" It's all right," Robert Blake assured him. " This lady wants to see the young gentleman whom she helped the other night."

The young gentleman, however, refused to take the slightest notice of her, and his mother was still brooding over the fact that " a leddy could be a doctor—and a good one, too."

Robert was waiting for her in the car and motored her along the road which had for her such strange memories.

" We'll park ' Biddy' here and go along the burn side," he said. The path was rough and it was necessary that he should give her

173

a helping hand. For some reason they were both conscious of a sense of restraint. Gone was all the gay badinage ; neither could think of a word to say.

"Let's sit down on this stone," Robert suggested.

"All right," she agreed. "You smoke ; I want to see if I can find a piece of sprouting bog-myrtle. It should be in the cone stage now."

"Don't fall into the burn, then," he warned her. "Hector is not here to save you as he did me, and my leg is groggy. In fact, if it were not for something Hector said to me the night he found me, I would not have had the courage to ask you to come here."

"What did Hector say ? " she asked, looking at him with startled eyes.

"He said you said : 'I'm trusting you, Hector, to find Robert Blake and bring him back to me.' That speech bucked me up, I can tell you. . . . So he brought me back to you, Elspet, and what have you to say about it ? "

Her lips were silent ; her eyes spoke volumes. She was half frightened when she saw the look of exultation on his face. It was *his* moment—the moment that comes in nearly every life when Heaven itself seems to have nothing better to offer us.

" If Hector hadn't told you, would you have kept silent ? " she asked.

He nodded.

" Then *I*'d have had to speak—how terrible!"

He agreed. " We owe a lot to Hector," he said fervently, and putting his arm round her he held her close. " And now let's stop speaking about him. Let's speak about ourselves."